Hope ya enjoy!

i

TALK MURDER TO ME

A novel by **Jack Terry**

She leaned in but instead of kissing me she pressed her lips to my ear. "Everybody reminds me of somebody, but you don't remind me of anybody. Why is that?" She stood back up and turned for the cabin hatch. "Is that because there's nobody like you in the world?"

It was funny. Rachel's parents had named her what they did because they were afraid that everybody reminded them of somebody, and she couldn't figure out why I didn't do the same. It was easy enough to explain: I was the flip side of the coin. I remind somebody of everybody.

I'm the older brother of your first high school girlfriend. I'm the guy who gave the toast at a wedding you were a guest at. I'm the man that held the door for you, sat next to you at the football game, even had a beer or two with you at the bar. I enter your conscious and exit your memory before I ever register. I'm a phantom, and even if I came face to face with someone whose very life had depended on what I told him, and he wanted to return the favor by making me chum, he would most likely buy me a drink and never remember who I was.

Talk Murder to Me

by

Jack Terry

Talk Murder To Me

Chapter 1

Take it from someone with recent experience: the last thing you want to have happen to you when you are coming back to reality, or at least what passes for it on your sun bleached little corner of the world, after a perfectly executed seven day stone, is to stumble upon a floater when you are trying to tie off your dinghy, because your first thought will be that you aren't quite done being stoned.

That was quite honestly my first concern. It might seem callous to some that I wasn't overly concerned about the body itself, but I recognized him right away. Name was Scooter, and he was at least forty years too old to be going by such a nickname. I'm not going to say anything like I'm glad he was dead or he got what he had coming to him – there were plenty of people who would be more than happy to say that and then some – but I sure as hell wasn't going to shed any tears for him. Here's everything you need to know about Scooter: I could barely stand to be in the same bar as him, and I was about the only person he considered a friend.

I'd seen enough dead bodies, floaters and otherwise, to be able to hazard a fair guess as to how long he had been gone. It was Monday now and he had the look of someone who had spent most of the weekend in the seawater. His mouth was kind of beat up, but there didn't seem to be any other bruising. Granted, he was still fully clothed, and I wasn't about to do anything to get a better look at him. Part of me felt like I had already seen too much. Thing is, how come no one else had?

Terry

It may have been early in the season but the tourists were here, and there were at least a half dozen boats that sailed off this dock on twice daily excursions. That means an easy 200 people had been tromping through here in the last couple of hours. Of course those that weren't hungover were the ones smart enough to be drinking again already, so observational skills were not at the forefront. Tourists are one thing, but locals are another and there were almost twenty dinghies already tied off by the live-aboards who had come in today. If he were as plain as day to me, then how the hell could everyone else have missed him? This meant there was only one conclusion: I was still stoned and he was a hallucination.

Problem is I wouldn't know for sure until something...well, happened. I didn't know what that would be. If we knew what we were going to hallucinate, it would take all the fun out of doing drugs in the first place. I finished tying off and kept watching him, convinced that he was a bad exclamation point at the end of what had been a mind blowing sentence, when a big old tarpon swam into view.

Tarpon really aren't much good for anything, except giving you the fight of your life on the open water. Most people find that hard to believe because the only tarpon they ever see are the fat lazy bastards scavenging around the docks. This one looked fatter and dumber than most, but I knew he was here to give me a sign. See, if Scooter wasn't really here, then the tarpon wasn't really here, and if the tarpon wasn't really here, that would make him a hallucination too, and as a hallucination he would be nice enough to tell me that, and I could get on with my day free and easy.

That fat dumb fish took one look at me and started nibbling Scooter's hair. Fuck.

Chapter 2

Like any good seedy falling down waterfront wreck of a bar in a drinking town with a tourist problem, Barnacle Bob's was already pleasantly full of people who didn't give a shit that it wasn't even noon somewhere, much less five o'clock. The good thing about most of the bartenders working is that they don't give a shit either. Some of the most successful bartenders I've met down here are done working by three in the afternoon. Of course that involves training yourself to be up before the crack of dawn, but local drunks are far better tippers and far less dramatic than out of town drunks. Or at least dramatic in a completely different way.

As soon as Candy – she's very defensive about that, swears she can even tell when someone speaks her name with an "I" at the end and not a "Y" – saw me swing my duffle onto the stool next to me and help myself to a cup of coffee, she left the south beach squadron to argue with themselves about the fact that all the drinks came in a plastic cup and began to set up my routine.

(Routine might not be the correct word. I don't want it to sound like I get stoned all the time. Fact is I rarely do, at least to the extent of the last seven days. I certainly drink a fair amount, and I usually have a joint or two every day, but the epic week-long adventures can only happen when several circumstances are just right. Maybe it's because they happen so rarely that they have become a routine. Or maybe Candy's just got a sharp memory.)

3

First up was a half a cup of OJ that went straight into my coffee. Next to that was a glass of red wine. Doesn't matter what kind, just as long as it's red. A bottle of Bud Light gets placed next to that, and the final step was a combination of shit tequila, peppermint schnapps and hot sauce chilled as cold as my ex-wife's heart. Candy was still shaking that up when Ryan came by with the oyster.

"You're on the ball today."

"Saw you sitting at the dock, figured you were coming up for this. What was attracting your attention down there anyway?"

"Your dignity?" Candy guessed as she poured the shot and Ryan added the oyster.

"Can't find what you never had."

"Maybe that's why I'm so attracted to you," she mused. "Mama always said I was drawn to the worst men for me."

"Baby," I replied as I lined up my recovery concoction, "I'm the best thing you've never had."

It's a matter of speed to make sure it all works right. You start by pounding the coffee. The OJ has chilled it enough so you can handle it, mostly. The shot comes right after that, oyster and all, and that is followed by the red wine, also gulped. It sounds horrible, and I guess it probably is if you stop to think about it, but that's the trick: no stopping, no thinking. Perhaps not the best motto for life, but sometimes it's what the doctor ordered. If it takes more than ten seconds you've probably screwed something up. But if you did it right, you'll know. As will everyone around you.

"Damn Tricky! A burp like that doesn't even sound human."

"Or smell human either." Ryan was already retreating to the kitchen.

"Maybe not, but it makes me feel like one again." Letting

go with such a belch is a great way to pick out the locals from the visitors, no matter how much they try to dress like each other. Locals go about like nothing has happened while the out of towners act like they just saw Jesus and Moses with their tongues down each other's throat. Most of them back away a few feet, but one of the people Candy had been arguing with earlier actually moved closer.

"What the hell kind of bar is this? No real glassware and slobs like that hanging out here. Shit man."

I knew what Candy wanted to say, but couldn't, for fear of her boss hearing her, so I said it for her. "It's the kind that doesn't give a fuck what MDT thinks about it."

"What the hell are you saying? MDT?"

I almost laughed and Candy walked away so she wouldn't be caught snickering herself. "Is this your first time in Key West?"

"Hell, no. We're here every few months. Is that okay with you?"

I ignored his question. "Nobody's ever called you MDT before?"

"No, and if it's an insult they'd be smart enough not to."

"Then I guess I'm just a dumb local." I went to my beer, figuring the conversation was over. The women he and his buddies were with were itching to go, or at least not be part of a scene, but he needed to prove himself to me.

"Maybe you're not as dumb as you look, seeing as how you still ain't told me what it means."

I thought for a second. "It's actually a badge of honor we give to some of our privileged visitors. Next bar you go to, you tell them Tricky Dick said you were MDT. They'll take good care of you."

I could tell he wasn't sure if he should believe me, but the voting public had spoken, five to zero with one abstention, that it was time to move on. He walked backwards with his group so I would know he was still speaking to me.

"If you're jerking my chain, I'll find out, and I'll find you. We're here for a week."

I let him go and just enjoyed my beer. Candy came back down my way, still laughing. I just shrugged. "What? Did you want me to invite him to stay for lunch?"

"You do live dangerously."

'Not as much as used to,' I thought to myself. Alienating strangers was nothing compared to the illustrious career I retired from a few years back. This was shooting baby fish in candy filled barrels compared to some of the shit I've dealt with.

Everything was doing its job, culminating with the beer settling my stomach and getting me ready for the day. The skies were bright and clear, the humidity was still missing, and I felt it was going to be a great day. The musician was setting up, and I thought maybe I'd change things up. The plan, as it always was, was to head over to the marina showers and wash off the last of the week, before heading back to the boat. I need to ease my way back into humanity, as my last run-in might have demonstrated to you. But the day was shaping up so perfect I might hit the shower and then spend a few hours sitting here thinking about all the things I didn't have to do. Just another nice relaxing...son of a bitch!

"Hey Candy, when was the last time you saw Scooter?"

"Friday, right as I was getting off."

Well, that sounds about right.

"You sure you didn't see him at any point over the weekend?"

"The miserable old goat? Every day I don't see him I stop at St. Mary's and light a candle of gratitude."

"Well, then I guess you better get me another beer for my shower before you call the cops."

"Cops? What the hell for?"

"He's what I was looking at under the dock." I grabbed the second beer and topped off my coffee.

"You sure you weren't still seeing things?"

"Nope. The tarpon would have told me."

"Son of a bitch." She punched the non-emergency numbers into the phone. "Where the hell are you going?"

"I just tag 'em. Let the cops bag him. He's right down there under the dock. Can't miss him." Well, apparently I can't, but nobody else had a problem walking right by him.

If this were a cartoon you'd see steam coming out of her ears while she waited for someone to answer. "If I gotta stay after my shift talking to these jag-off cops I'm gonna shit. It's my fucking Friday!"

Good ole' Scooter. Three days dead and still pissing people off.

Terry

Chapter 3

It may seem romantic and mystical to live on a sailboat. Ask anyone who works middle management or calls a cubicle farm home in the middle of winter where they'd rather be, and a lot of them will say anchored in some palm tree lined harbor watching the sunset. People always fantasize about that stuff, but what they don't consider is the dreary day to day (or every few days) stuff like getting clean. That's why God created marinas. Think of them as truck stops for sailboats. You can get supplies, fuel, something to eat and they have laundry facilities and showers.

I felt like a new man after I was clean and decided that the new man should have a new plan. I know you may find this hard to believe, but I didn't just get stoned for seven days because it was fun. There's a deeper connection that I'm going for there, some way to let the universe help me with my problems. You might think I swallowed a few too many new age and astrology books, but when you think about it, we all have certain things that help us make sense of our lives. My things just happen to include full moons, peyote and a talking manatee.

That beautiful day was calling my name and so I figured I'd start by heading back to Barnacle Bob's. If nothing else I could at least have a beer while listening to Candy tell the story about the cops.

The first indication that there might be a problem was there were no cops to be seen. No yellow crime scene tape, no body getting removed from the water, not even a guy with a megaphone urging people to move along because there was nothing to see here. I was pretty sure I'd seen Candy talking on the phone, but I figured maybe I should check in with her about that.

"If it had been somebody the cops actually gave a shit about, they would have busted a hump getting here." I witnessed the angriest bottle opening in the world. "Him being who he was, once they found out he wasn't in any danger of drifting away they made some vague promises about showing up within the hour."

She was pissed off enough to not want to talk about it, and I was stymied enough to not know what to do. I may have liked Scooter as much as the next guy when he was alive, which is to say not very much, and there is probably nothing the least bit curious about how he ended up there, but there was something gnawing at me. The truth is it felt disrespectful, regardless of who it was, to just leave a dead man lying there. I caught Candy's eye. "Let me have another and I'm going to go keep him company until the cavalry arrives."

"Trying to be a nice guy, or trying to make sure he's still there?"

I didn't have to say anything for her to know the answer was centrally located in option B, so I just paid for my morning libations and headed back to the dock. But yeah, before I got too comfortable, I poked my head over the side. The tarpon was gone, but his morning nosh was still there.

The good thing about the delay was it gave me some time to review the last seven days. When I say that it was an executed stone, I mean it. This wasn't bong-hits-and-cough-syrup-with-six-of-your-friends getting stoned. This was a carefully planned out adventure, with built in plateaus and periods of reflection, all structured to peak about five and a half days in. If I time it right, the apex of it all starts with the sunset on the day of the full moon. Not just any moon but one of those super moons with the major high tide. I ride that sensation in the pulpit of my sailboat until just about sunrise.

Obviously such high tides are rare, so that's one of the reasons I don't do it as often as Candy and Ryan's preparations may lead you to believe. It seems that in a world full of so-called automated precision, the most accurate thing I have found is something purely natural. The peyote I take lasts the same amount of time every time. It starts to kick in right as the sun is saying good bye and finishes wearing off by the time it shows back up on the other horizon. The first time it wore off it was still dark out but there were enough other elements I had at my disposal to get me through until the sunrise so I didn't become too paranoid. I wasn't so lucky the second time. Let me tell you nothing sucks more than to still be ball deep on the peyote when it has become full daylight. Made me question everything.

Ironically questioning anything at this point isn't too bright a plan. It's important to not question the process too much afterwards, because once you do you start to doubt exactly what the manatee meant when the two of you were talking. See, if I question all of this after the fact, I'm far too rational a guy to start with any thought other than 'Of course he wasn't *really* talking to me.' At that point the best I can salvage it with is to say he was talking to nature and the universe as a whole, and I just happened to be there, but let's face it: if the manatee is not going to talk directly to you, then why waste the time on the peyote in the first place? You doubt the manatee, you doubt everything, and the trip becomes meaningless.

Unlike my first run in with Scooter this morning, there were two facts I was sure of when I was talking to the manatee the night before last. Fact one was that he was real, and fact two was that I was stoned. I have already explained how I know fact two is true, and as for fact one, he's been keeping me company on and off for several months now. I don't understand why. I mean, I know I'm a charming guy and all that, but my boat is pretty far out in the mooring field, with no food around for him. Still, there's something about me he likes, because he keeps coming back for more.

I actually didn't see him the other night when we were talking. I was lying on the pulpit watching the moon when I felt the boat begin to shake. The nudge was too perfect, too precise, and too manatee-ish to be a result of the tide. I called out to him so he would know I was up front. He swam out and (I'm speculating here) floated onto his back so he could see the moon as well. If he hadn't, his mouth would've been in the water and all I would have heard were bubbles. He obviously wasn't seeing the same moon I was looking at, but I guess that's what you get by shunning responsibility, forgoing society and spending your days in warm ocean water. Even with all the drugs in the world, I'll never be able to see nature as beautifully as animals do.

We talked a lot, sometimes out loud and other times just in thoughts, and he helped me understand much that I was missing. It's nice to have someone to check in with every once in a while, you know, to help keep my head on straight.

I just wish he could have told me about the black panties I found on deck.

Chapter 4

I had finished the new beer and was debating the merits of another versus the benefits of a nap in the sun when the sound of two self-confident man-children caught my attention. Key West's third finest, from the looks of it.

"That's all the reported passing of Scooter warrants? If you two are here, who's directing traffic?"

"Traffic detail rotates, and you know that Tricky." Our first speaker is Maples, a competent if a little too literally minded fellow who takes his job far more seriously than most. His family's been living on the island for eight generations now. Legend has it that some ancestor was so full of himself that he refused to live anywhere where trees with his name outnumbered his family. There were many places he could have dragged his family, I guess, but probably didn't feel like hedging his bets "Besides we were told to make sure that it was actually Scooter and that he was actually dead."

Somehow that made up my mind for me. I closed my eyes and I leaned my head back against the piling. "It's a sad day when the chief forgets our long standing history and no longer trusts my judgement."

"Funny you should mention that." Suarez is Jeff to Maples' Mutt, not as intense but no less committed to his job. Anything else Suarez was going to say sounded like it got cut off by a slap to the gut from Maples. "Are you going to help us look for your dear departed friend?"

12

"Hold on to a piling, lean over the edge and look in the water underneath it. First dead body you see is probably him."

I heard the sound of moving feet followed by what I thought would be several minutes of blissful silence. Instead a piercing whistle shot through my ears.

"What the fuck?"

"That's our question for you sleeping beauty. We seem to be missing something here."

"Seriously. He's two hundred pounds of dead flesh. How can you be missing him?"

"Why don't you just come down here and show us what we can't see?"

Son of a bitch. Maybe the tarpon not talking had nothing to do with how stoned I may or may not have been. This would look bad on me, but sure enough when I joined them, Scooter was nowhere to be seen.

"I swear he was right here when I tied off this morning. And after I came back from the shower and the bar, he was right where I left him."

"At the bar, huh? Glad to see you have your priorities straight."

"How else was I going to call you?"

"With your cell phone like everyone else." Maples spoke with a smile, before adding "Oh, wait..."

Suarez looked like he'd just eaten a lemon. "You don't have a phone?"

"Strange concept, I know, but part of the reason I moved to the end of the world was so I wouldn't be bothered by telemarketers." By this point I had laid myself down and was leaning over the water. "Just hold your Johnsons for a second."

Years of opening my eyes in the ocean had prepared me

for the fact that it still hurt like hell. The water was clear enough for me to see that Scooter had drifted about halfway under the dock. I was kind of surprised he hadn't kept going right out the other side, but that was when I noticed the handiwork. Somebody had made quite an effort to guarantee he didn't get too far away. I couldn't reach the body, but I could reach the rope.

I popped my head out of the water right before Scooter did, causing my friends in blue to jump back in alarm. "Don't ever doubt me again, boys." Seven days of doing less than nothing made me easily winded, so I flopped on my back while they wrestled with the body. They got about half of him on the dock, but whatever was anchoring that rope was not moving for them. The two of them looked at each other and then at me. I pulled out my knife and stuck my head back underwater.

Once the body was free and they were radioing in that I was not, in fact, full of shit, I figured my good deed for the day was over and I went to the bar. A cold beer was waiting for me but I didn't have much time to enjoy it before Suarez was standing next to me.

"You here to give me the key to the city for being such a responsible citizen?"

"Well, for starters we're going to need you to fill out a report."

"Yeah? Here's my report. I came in, I tied off, I saw the body, and I called you. End of report."

"That's only part of it though. The chief wants to meet with you. The new chief."

The bottle of beer was pressed to my lips but I was too busy swallowing what he had just said to drink anymore. The corner of my mouth moved. "Whaddya mean, new chief?"

"Just what I said. Four days ago."

"What the fuck happened?"

"I don't know man." Nothing I hate more than watching a painfully honest cop try to explain an obviously crooked situation. "One day it's him, the next day it's not. Nobody's saying nothing."

"But they can't just switch the chief of police like that, with no public notification or anything."

"You want to make a list of all the things you can't do on the mainland that are S.O.P. down here, we'll be writing until dinnertime. But it's done and you better show. He asked for you by name."

I threw some money on the bar. "Which one of you noobs told him my real name?"

"Nobody did. Dispatch said 'Tricky Dick's got a floater,' and before anything else could be said he called out your full name. He even knew about Tricky Ti...about your other nickname."

Only one other person calls me by that name, at least to my face. If he knows that name, he probably knows her, and if he does, I'm in for a bad day.

Chapter 5

I don't believe in God. Maybe I did at one point, a long time ago, but I have seen too many things happen to too many people in too many places between then and now to believe anymore. Problem is, I think God believes in me, and he is hell-bent on making me believe in him.

He doesn't do this by creating miracles or fulfilling promises though. He does it by making things happen that fuck my life up so completely and unpredictably that there is no way it is a coincidence or dumb luck or bad timing or anything else. They are certain things no human could possibly be responsible for. So it was that morning that my faith in faithlessness was put to its strictest test in a very long time. How else could I explain the presence of the one person I truly, completely and totally hate was now the Key West Chief of police.

"Do you know how many years I spent walking through swamps, flipping over rocks, just to see if I could find the one you scurried under? And here you are, living in paradise." In case you didn't pick up on it, he's not too fond of me either.

"Fuck you."

"Such language. I could have you arrested."

"Wish I'd known. I would have skipped the shower and had one on the city's dime."

His effort to look genuinely hurt would have been more effective if he wasn't trying mightily to contain his laughter. "We can try this greeting again if you want. I mean, are you sure you want those to be the first words you say to me, after all these years? If I remember right, they were the last words you said to me as well."

"I was kind of hoping they'd be the last words I would ever say to you."

"And yet here we are. So I guess we better both make the best of it."

"What happened to Chief Phillips?"

"Family emergency, had to retire immediately."

"Bull shit."

"He contracted a terrible disease, had to retire immediately."

"Bull shit."

"He got tired of you, had to retire immediately."

"You know I can find out."

All sense of humor flooded out of the room, and he was the sketchy bastard I had grown to hate. "I thought you didn't want to find out. I thought that was why you started 'distancing' yourself from the life you had. Word around the water cooler is you managed to put all of your past behind you and become some sort of eco-friendly peace loving, got a smile for everyone wunderkind who got lost on his way home from Woodstock. To find out about your old friend, who I assure you is perfectly fine, would involve going back into that world. And on the list of things I know, I know doing that is the last thing you want." He got up and sat on the corner of the desk, giving himself an even more superior angle on me. "And I know that if you even try, the most miserable existence you can imagine would look like a Shangri-La compared to where I would make sure you end up. All you need to know is that I'm your new Chief of police."

The adrenaline coursed through my body, driving away

the beers, the shots, the last seven days, the last several years. I hadn't felt like this in a long time. It felt good. I didn't like it, but I found myself craving it. I got up from the chair, riding my energy in a casual ramble around the office.

"Nothing says I have to stay. I could just pull up anchor and go."

This brought the laughter back in the room, but it was not the kind you'd hear at a children's party. "Go where? You don't want to go back up north, and there isn't a country south of here that would let you use their toilet, much less call it home."

"Doesn't matter. I'm a quiet law abiding citizen." (Mostly.) "I won't have to ever see you."

"Well, now that's going to be hard to do," he said as he moved back to his chair, "considering you're going to be working for me again."

This was why I may have been craving it but I didn't like it. It made me want to react. If I had been talking to almost anyone else, my reaction would have already happened and my point would have been made. The thing is, he knew exactly what I was feeling, he knew exactly what my reaction would be, and he would be exactly one step ahead of me the whole time. That was why I had crawled away from him, and that was why he had let me go. Because he knew that one day he would need this.

"What if I say no?"

"You can say it all you want. It doesn't matter. The choice isn't up to you. You're the guy I need for this job. Hell, and it pains me to say this, even if it hadn't been your washed up soul that found his washed up body, I still might have tracked you down for this."

"There's nothing you can do to force me."

"I can make your life hell."

"You already did."

"That was your old life. How about this new life of yours? I'm sure you enjoy your new life out there on your boat as a (mostly) law-abiding citizen. I would sure hate to see anything happen to that."

I laughed out of genuine surprise and amusement. "Really? You think you can mess with me and my boat? I'm not sure what kind of crash course they gave you on your way through the remedial edition of the Police Academy, but let me fill you in on how things work. First of all, the Coast Guard is King Shit of the water around these parts. That is of course when the Navy has no use for it. Secondly, the mooring field is overseen by the county and not the city. So if you want to come out to my boat and swing your dick around, showing me how tough you are, you better get in line. Now, are you going to arrest me so I can get my bonus shower, or am I free to go?"

His expression didn't change. It should have bothered me but it didn't. That was an oversight I would eventually pay for. He got up from his desk like a dutiful host and opened the door for me. "You're free to do whatever you like with your life."

"Thank you. That's all I've wanted." I walked outside thinking that maybe it was back to being a good day to wake up to after all.

Terry

Chapter 6

Visiting with people I hated usually did a number on my appetite, and it dawned on me the closest thing I've had to food so far today was the oyster swimming in the tequila. The Pelican Deck has one hell of a pulled pork sandwich and I knew Yeddie would be working.

Nicknames aren't all they're cracked up to be. Nobody gets to choose their own nickname. Instead they are given to you by your peers, which mean the circumstances leading up to them might not be one a person wants to continually recall. This was just one of the reasons Yeddie was a great dude.

Once upon a time his name had been Edward. As a child he had been a terrific kid, naturally curious and a little roly-poly (that's what he tells us anyway) and no one could call him anything but Eddie. When puberty hit, it hit with a vengeance. By the time it was all said and done, he was 6'10" and built like a house. He tried to work out as much as he could, to keep from being roly-poly forever, but it was a struggle keeping up with how fast he was growing. He ended up as an adult being an only slightly more slender but ridiculously taller version of himself as a kid. Thing is, his size is the second most remarkable physical attribute he has.

Eddie's an albino.

If you're like anyone with half a brain, you might wonder why someone who doesn't handle the sun so well would choose a subtropical island as their new home. Like most people do after a few rounds, you might even ask. Surely you think there has to be a deep conversation, a family history, a broken heart, something.

Nope. He just says "Everybody's gotta live somewhere."

I can't fault logic I don't understand, so I settle for amusing myself by watching the confused expressions on people's faces. Mostly they let it go, but some people push the issue, looking for clarification that isn't there. A few even go over the top (which just goes to show how drunk they are. I mean, the guy is 6'10" and the size of a house) but one day, one drunken putz took it all the way to Mount Everest.

"Man, you have got to be like the biggest albino, like...ever." The kid was twenty-one and a day, and apparently never learned how to handle his liquor ahead of time like most kids. Whatever cool he had been trying to show was gone. "And you are probably the only fucking albino on the island. That makes you double rare." Eddie did what he always did when somebody wouldn't let it go; he smiled and kept working. "I mean, you're like Bigfoot and the Loch Ness monster had a kid rare." Some of us were starting to get edgy. As big as Eddie was, he didn't have a mean streak in his body, but we were plenty mean enough to make up for it if this kid got any more out of line.

"You're even rarer than that, man! You're like, you're like, the abominable snowman dude, you know that thing, what'd they call him, what'd they call him?"

The kid had a few buddies with him who were as unimpressed with him as we were. One of the kids mouthed the answer, hoping it would shut him up.

"That's it man! You're like the Yeti!"

Eddie froze.

The kid didn't know Eddie. The kid probably didn't even know who he was. He sure as shit was too drunk to have remembered his name, if he had even heard it. All we knew

21

is the kid would probably wake up tomorrow in some overcrowded hotel room, too hungover to remember most of what he had done the night before. But we all knew Eddie, and we all one thought:

How the fuck had we not thought of that ourselves?

Two minutes ago we were all ready to toss the kid out on his ear, and now we wanted to make him an honorary member of our club. I think the only thing that kept us from laughing – and thereby allowing us to keep drinking at the Pelican – was we saw that Eddie was still frozen. We may have been wrong about him not having a mean streak in him, because when he finally moved again, he did so very deliberately towards the kid's friends.

"I think your buddy has had enough to drink, and I think he's leaving. Right. Now."

He was right. They did. He started coming back down the bar towards us and we all suddenly had something far more important to look at than him. We'd eventually hear through the grapevine that the kid would end up passing out at Denny's before throwing up in a taxi and being on the hook for a hundred dollar cleaning fee, but right then all we could think about was how Eddie was going to react. He just went about his job for a couple of minutes before he started to laugh.

"Yeddie." He thought about it for a second. "Hell, I've been called worse."

Maybe so, but I can guarantee you that since that day he hasn't been called anything else.

Chapter 7

"You having lunch today?"

"Yup."

He typed in the order and poured us each a shot before leaning against the beer cooler.

"Slow day."

"One ship didn't come in and the other is full of krauts that leaves at 5."

"Fun, fun."

"Another day in paradise. Cheers."

Smooooooooooooooth.

"Heard you found Scooter face down at the dinghy dock this morning."

"Word travels fast."

"Small island, big mouths. Any idea who did it?"

"No, but I know about a couple thousand who probably wanted to."

Some out of towners with their hands full of coupons sat at the other end of the bar and Yeddie left me with this pearl of wisdom. "At least we know he'll have a big funeral. Everyone is gonna show up just to make sure he's really dead."

Funny thing was that Yeddie was probably more right than he knew. As a matter of fact it would most likely turn out to be the biggest party on the island in quite a time, if you don't count all the activities the tourism commission puts on for the visitors. For such a small island it seems pretty easy to fall into the same routines. I could go months without seeing people I've known since I first moved down here and then one night just bump into them. The upside is that when that happens it's like no time has passed. That's what would make Scooter's funeral such a good time. Everybody would start with stories bitching about him, but within five minutes we'd all be reliving the good times, even the ones he was part of.

I think there were two.

I should have been paying better attention to my surroundings than I was. That way I would have seen the crazy Canuck and made myself scarce. He snuck up on me and next thing I knew he was breathing in my face.

"Hey Tricky, I hear it was your rod that pulled up Scooter today."

We called him the crazy Canuck for two reasons. He was Canadian, and he was battier than a shit-house rat.

"Just stumbled upon him when I was tying off. Dumb luck."

"Yeah, maybe it was, maybe it was, just like maybe it was dumb luck that it was his time to die."

"I don't know about that. Seemed like more than just luck was involved."

He started cackling in a way that reminded me of the cheesiest kids in the worst drive-in horror movies. "That's right, that's right, it's not luck to die when somebody wants you dead. I know it wasn't luck."

"Mmm-hmmm, probably because I just told you that."

"You think that Trick, do you? You do? What if I told you I knew it wasn't luck before I even talked to you?"

"I'd say you're full of crap."

Yeddie had finished redeeming coupons and came over to watch the floor show.

"What's the Canuck up to?"

"I don't know, but I think he's trying to enlighten me in the ways of murder."

He slapped a couple of grimy bucks on the bar, the going rate for a local's draft. "Oh I am, I am. See, I knew Scooter was dead before you did, or you did, or any of you did."

"Well, then why did you leave me the trouble of calling the police?"

"That's just it Tricky, that's it. I didn't want no trouble."

"Yeah? Why's that?"

"I's the one that made sure he was dead."

If reason number one for not wanting to help out the Chief was because I hated him with a passion, reason one-A was because I knew this was what was gonna happen as word got around town. Every asshole on the island that ever had a run-in with Scooter would have an alibi. Not for why they couldn't have been the murderer, but for how they were there when it happened. I figured no time like the present to start spreading the word my involvement with Scooter was over.

"Why you telling me Crazy? You really think I care?"

"Don't you want to hear how I did it?"

"Not in the least."

"I do." Yeddie was giggling because he knew as well as I that there was no way Crazy could've killed anyone. "This could be funny."

"You want funny? Listen to this." I turned to face the Canuck. "Up in the Great White North, they got Boy Scouts?"

"Of course they do."

"Were you ever one?"

"Hell no."

"Hmmmm." I posed as if I were deep in thought. "And if I remember, you ain't much of a fisherman, are you?"

25

He just cackled again.

"So that makes me wonder how it was you came to be so good at tying knots."

"Who said I was?"

"Yeah, I mean you strike me as the type of guy who probably even has a hard time tying his shoes."

"Ha! Shows you what you know!" He pointed to his feet. "Flip flops!"

"That's what I thought." My food showed up and I swiveled back toward the bar. I gave the sandwich my undivided attention until the Canuck couldn't take anymore.

"Thought what?"

"That you didn't have a damn thing to do with Scooter getting killed, and you know it. Now if you excuse me, I'm trying to eat and you – you make that hard to do."

It's hard to imagine how a rattling bag of crazy bones can move the way he does, but he slunk off as quietly as he had snuck up. Yeddie was more confused than amused.

"What does knot tying have to do with any of it?"

"Whoever killed him tied him off to some serious piece of anchor so the body wouldn't float away."

"That's fucked up." Service tickets started to print up and he began to make drinks. "Seems like a dumb thing to do to something that you want to keep hidden."

That's what was scaring me. Whoever killed Scooter didn't want to hide him.

They wanted him to be found.

Chapter 8

The run in with the dead body, the police and the Canuck notwithstanding, this was still turning out to be a pretty good day. Maybe in the future I'd have to make this exception the rule. While I was eating lunch Jack Seemiller had taken the stage and he was great at getting a crowd going. Between the hot music and the cold beer, it was easy for me to enjoy the afternoon.

In spite of what impression you may have gotten from me and the Chief talking, I really am a very easy going guy. It took me a long time to get there, and it is something I struggle with every day – I may have retired early, but just like anyone else I didn't shrug all that off in a day. Maybe that was what the Chief was talking about when he said I was the guy he needed for this. He hated that about me in the past, my ability to keep things separate, to seemingly walk away from stress, but maybe now it would be a benefit. I couldn't see how, but within an hour of being at the bar I couldn't care either.

I left as Jack was finishing up, tossing a twenty and a beer in his tip jar. It had been a full and fun day, in so many strange ways, but it was time to get back home, watch the sunset, and slip into a peaceful, reasonably untroubled sleep. I was halfway to my boat when I thought that might not happen.

From a distance I thought that whoever she was, she might be related to Yeddie. When I finished tying off to my

only pair, but I tilted my head as if I was trying to look up her thighs. An eyebrow cocked over the top of her glasses.

"You looking for anything special?"

She spoke first. Score one for me.

"I'm just wondering if you're here because you miss me, or because you're out of clean laundry."

"Wouldn't matter if I was. I doubt you washed them for me." She paused when she looked me over. "Cleanliness doesn't seem to be too far up your list of priorities."

What? She couldn't tell I showered? Hell, if I was right, I was a damn sight cleaner than the last time she saw me. "They say it's next to Godliness, and since He and I don't see eye to eye on too many things, I feel no special need to focus on it."

Her response was to purse her lips and look out over the harbor. To make sure she kept my attention, she re-crossed her legs, slowly enough to let me know that she was in no hurry for what she left behind, and that black was indeed her favorite color.

"They're on top of the cabin, right next to the stairs."

Her eyes came back to me, and the eyebrow cocked again. Right. It's up to me to get them. Sure. Who does she think I am? It takes more than a pretty smile and long legs to make me jump.

So why did I find myself standing there with a pair of black panties in my hands? Son of a bitch...

Terry

Chapter 9

She steered her dinghy with one hand, a cocktail and her panties in the other. I sat in the bow, watching the world go by in the short trip between boats. It doesn't matter how often I am on the water, nothing is more exciting for me than to watch. This is the view that led me to drop my anchor here, not some woman. Besides, I figured I was going to have at least a few hours to look at her.

"I hope you're hungry," she said as we climbed onboard.

"To be honest, not very. I've settled into the one meal a day lifestyle."

"Well, too bad, because I promised I'd make you dinner, and I never go against my promises."

"That's fine with me, then." I had no idea what she was talking about, but I'm guessing it was part of the conversation we had before she took her panties off. Or maybe it was afterwards, when she was getting ready to leave, and felt like she owed me. Nah, that didn't make any sense. It must have been before.

Her boat was far too nice to be moored out in what was basically a floating graveyard, or at least a nautical hospice. In theory, every boat is inspected by the Coast Guard once a year to prove that it is actually still a boat. The reality is that many people here treat their boats much like their cousins do the double-wides back home. Technically those are trailers, but everyone knows the only time they move is when a tornado tells them to. Mostly people make the most perfunctory repairs and remodels to their boats, giving the

30

illusion of seaworthiness, cross their fingers and turn the other way. As long as no hurricanes come to wipe the slate clean, nobody's the wiser.

"You sure you shouldn't be docking this somewhere nicer than this long term economy lot?"

"If I did that I never would have the chance to meet such interesting people like you." She had a small grill going, but whatever she was making did not smell like your typical burger.

"This is Key West honey. You can't swing a dead iguana without hitting a half dozen 'interesting' people."

She turned the heat down and moved over to sit across from me. We had switched from tequila to Tempranillo and she topped off my glass before she sat. "I looked at some of the slips, but it felt like the difference between buying a house and living in an apartment. Out here there's a little more space between everyone."

"Yeah but it's a bitch when you try to mow the lawn."

She laughed, but the smile it quickly settled into seemed a little disjointed. Something was lurking behind it, and I didn't feel like I wanted to know exactly what it was.

"And being out here on your own, it isn't so safe. Some of the people out here are pretty sketchy."

"Do I look like someone who should be worried?"

"You don't know these people."

"They don't know me." She handed me her empty glass. "Excuse me while I slip into my dining attire."

"I didn't know this was going to be fancy dress."

She spoke over her shoulder as she headed down the stairs. "I'm sure you're wearing about the fanciest thing you own."

I thought about how Scooter had been tied up under the water, and I wasn't sure if she knew that's how sketchy these people could be. Come to think of it, I didn't know if they could be that sketchy. People out here shoot someone because they refuse to share a beer with them, or they torch a boat after someone insults them. Reactionary stuff, things that almost make sense to someone whose world has been simmering in the slow bake oven of the tropics for the last thirty years marinating in booze. Whatever happened to Scooter had been planned in advance, and maybe he himself had been sketchy enough to deserve it.

The more pressing issue than the dead guy in the water was the live woman on the boat, and I tried to figure out who she was and when I met her. Seven days of being stoned will do that to you, collateral damage for realigning with the cosmos. I was wracking my brain when I felt three familiar bumps on the side of the boat. I looked over the railing to see a friendly face.

"I am glad to see you!"

"Saw you get in the dinghy with that dumb look on your face."

"I've been practicing it for years. When did I meet her?"

"Two moons before the full one. You were dancing to the sunset and she came over to see the show up close."

Quickly it came back to me in flashes. Her coming on board and giggling at my interpretive sunset dance, me finally putting on a pair of shorts at her insistence, us snacking and drinking, me counting the stars while she did something else, and her flinging her panties at me before leading me down to my cabin. Only one thing wasn't flashing, and it was kind of important.

"What the hell is her name?"

"Are you kidding? I don't even know yours."

The boat shifted and I knew she was coming back up the stairs. He gave me a flipper wave as he rolled over and slid beneath the waves, and I had just enough time to stand up and act casual.

Turns out black wasn't the only color she owned. A pair of white capris accentuated the slate gray blouse she had on, barely, as it seemed determined to redefine what off the shoulder fashion meant. That alabaster skin was smooth and even, making me wonder how many digits were in the SPF of her sunblock. When people think about no tan lines, they usually picture an even tan that never stops. She took it the other direction and I sure wish I could remember what her lack of tan lines looked like.

She joined me on the rail. "Talking to your friend again?"

Shit. She must have been something special, or I must have been somewhere special if I told her about the manatee. At this point I decided the best offense was to punt, give her the ball and let my team regroup. "Yeah, I was hoping he could answer some questions for me."

"Like the ones he was going to help with you with during the full moon?"

"No, nothing so galactic and esoteric. Smaller stuff, quality of life type things."

"Like how we met and what my name is?"

"Get out of my head woman! Were you listening?"

She laughed again, and this time it seemed relaxed, more genuine. "You made a very specific point the other night of telling me that, how did you put it, 'as astounding as I was, your mental damn was not retaining anything tonight'."

"Yeah that sounds like me. So I guess you know what my next question is going to be..."

"In time." She handed me a pipe and a bag. "You should probably relax a little first."

I packed the bowl and offered it to her first, but she demurred. "Can't. I have work to do in Miami tomorrow."

"So, what? You just want me to smoke?"

"You need it. If I remember right, you're far more interesting when you're stoned."

Chapter 10

I've been called a lot of things in my life. Interesting has usually been near the top of the list, and frankly it hasn't been one of my favorites. First of all, it's a pretty subjective word. What is interesting to me may be dull as dishwater to you. Far more important is the fact that when someone calls me interesting, my initial thought is what did I do to make them think that? What made me successful with what I've done in my life is by being as low-key as possible. Compared to what I was like before I was retired I'm a social butterfly these days. Yet this was the second time she called me that in about ten minutes. Maybe she was just saying it because it struck her as funny, or maybe there was a lot more to what I don't remember and what I might have said during that time. Instead of pushing the issue and tipping my hand I decided to switch the focus on to her.

"What kind of work do you do? Or did we cover that already?"

"We did not. I work in fashion and publicity."

"Meaning."

"Meaning I write articles for magazines and websites, and I also consult with private labels to help them with their marketing."

"Explains the wardrobe you have. Although I don't know if it would qualify as fashion here in the tropics, or even Miami." I put the pipe down and leaned back in the chair. "But I could certainly see how smoking pot tonight might screw up your fashion sense tomorrow."

35

"I have recently seen what smoking too close to an important event can do to a person."

"Don't judge what you don't know about."

"So enlighten me then. Tell me about your special activity."

People always say that it's too hard to explain something when the truth is they just don't feel like talking about it. You can trust me when I say that my life is too hard to explain. I may look young but that's partially because I was able to retire early from a long and anonymous career. When I retired there were new things I wanted to learn and old things I wanted to forget.

"There is so much of the brain that we 'don't use.' Truth is we use it, but we just don't know how or why. Whenever the situation is right, I simply try to find a new way to tap into it. And I figure if I'm going to do it, why not incorporate nature as well? Worked well enough for other situations, so maybe it'll be good enough for me."

I'm sorry if it sounds like a prepared speech, but that's exactly what it is. It's one I've been working on for a while but never really have a chance to use. I call it speech "A." The few times I have said it in the past I was greeted by people nodding, smiling and backing away slowly. Speech "B" is a lot shorter, but I didn't think me saying "I like getting stoned" would fly with her.

"Do you think following the practices of civilizations that no longer exist is all that smart? Obviously they didn't know what they were doing."

"What they didn't know was smallpox."

I could tell she was weighing whether or not to start a sociological/historical debate about colonialism, but the decision was made for her by the grill. Dinner – a casual seafood stew served with rice and more wine – was ready, and we ate in near silence. It can be hard to move from a heavy topic like cultural genocide to something like "How do you think the Marlins will do this year?" and when we finished eating I honestly wasn't sure which topic would be less enjoyable. I took her empty plate with mine and set them on the table. Grabbing a new bottle of wine I didn't return to her but made my way to the bow. It may set every day and it may set everywhere, but it is still beautiful to watch.

When she figured I wasn't coming back she joined me and we watched in silence. Just as it disappeared she started to speak but I held up a finger. "Listen."

"To what?"

I didn't have to say anything. If you didn't know what you were listening for, you probably wouldn't be able to figure out what the noise was. It was kind of like a buzzing, or the wind blowing against some leaves. Hell, if the wind was blowing the wrong way you wouldn't be able to hear it at all. Today it was blowing as if the sun itself had set it free and the culmination of the applause made it to our ears. When it finally died away I asked her what she was going to say.

"Another one of your ritual celebrations?"

"We take what little things we can, because we never know when we can take them again."

The look she gave me before she got up and headed back to the stern told me which way the conversation was going to go. I just hoped I hadn't started pushing it there the first night we met.

Had I been too heavy? Did I let something slip I shouldn't have? You can only have so many lies to keep track of and too many truths you keep hidden before cracks start to appear. Most cases – the cases I've been getting used to anyway – it would just take a joke, a drink, or a misdirection, but not this woman. I could tell she would be smart enough to see through it, and I wasn't dumb enough to let her. I needed to pull out something special.

I stood up and saw that she had sat with her back to me, so without any fanfare I started taking off my clothes. The sky was still glowing enough in the post sunset gloaming that if anyone was looking they would be treated to one hell of a show, but I was only thinking about my audience of one. I took the time to neatly fold my clothes and form a nice stack with them. I dropped them on the seat next to her when I got to the stern. She looked up at me.

"What did I do to deserve this?"

"If I remember right, it's what you found interesting about me in the first place." She stifled a giggle as I stepped in closer. "And if I remember right, you're far more interesting when your mouth is full."

Chapter 11

Things that mess me up first thing in the morning:
1) Waking up in a strange bed.
2) Waking up alone in a strange bed.
3) Waking up alone and naked in a strange bed.

Luckily I could address at least one of those concerns. Unless something had been done to them during the course of the night, my clothes should still be piled up on the bench at the top of the stairs. Taking care of finding them would alleviate the other two situations, so I rationalized that's what I should do.

I really didn't remember if she was more interesting with her mouth full or not, but it had definitely been a much more memorable night in general. Turns out she was interesting in many different ways. I don't know how late it was when we finally made it below deck, but I do know we made several pleasurable stops along the way.

The light streaming in through the port hole showed me that a repeat appearance of me sans wardrobe had the potential of being a far better attended performance than the night before, but looking around told me I didn't have much of a choice. Apparently being in fashion meant you couldn't leave a spare towel lying around. I could hear her footsteps above me, so I figured there was no time like the present. I rolled out of bed and went above deck, head held high and hands held low.

She took one look at me and I realized my hands were not covering nearly enough. "I thought you said you weren't a morning person."

"That's the only part of me that is."

"Surprised you have any stamina left."

"It's more like an involuntary reaction.

She grabbed hold of it right before it disappeared into my shorts. "Would hate to have this go to waste."

"Funny, I was thinking the same thing."

She wrapped her other arm around my neck, letting her robe fall open. Her touch was deliberate and I was afraid that in a few more seconds I'd have nothing else left to think about. Turns out she was several steps ahead of me.

"Too bad you don't have time." Just as quickly she pulled her hands back, closed her robe and sat down. "Looks like I'm not the only one interested in you this morning."

Blood was flowing in all sorts of wrong directions, but I managed to pull focus and follow her gaze. The Coast Guard had pulled up to my boat and was looking to see if anyone was home.

"What the hell? They already woke me up yesterday."

"Excuse me?"

"Long story. I better get over there. Fire up the dinghy."

"Excuse me?!"

"What? I need to get over there."

"And I need to get ready for work. And you kept talking last night about how much you love the ocean. Now looks like the perfect time for that love. Besides," she stood up and crossed over to head below deck, giving me one last stroke, "this will serve as the perfect rudder."

Chapter 12

The truth is it's not really a long story as much as it is a confusing one. What you need to understand is that what passes for normal down here would be unheard of anywhere else, and what could get you arrested for in the rest of the world may actually earn you "citizen of the day" and a parade in your honor. It's like Suarez said: standard operating procedure ain't so standard here at the end of the road. Part of the charm. So, yeah, I have the Coast Guard serve as my wake-up call once in a while.

I told you there were several factors that go into the planning. One of them is knowing when my nephew is working. Technically he's an old friend's daughter's husband, but you know how those things go. I trust myself and what I'm doing enough to know I'll be fine, but it helps to have a familiar face in a uniform to make sure I'm breathing and let me know I've come back to reality.

Usually it's an unnecessary precaution, and yesterday was no exception. By the time he showed up I was already sitting on the deck, one eye closed, and enough coffee for the crew lucky enough to be with him.

"Good morning Commandant."

"I see I've earned a promotion."

"Think of it as an honorary title."

"Kind of like being called the mayor but not having the keys to city hall?"

"Exactly. Time for a few questions."

"Shoot."

Terry

"How many guys are here with me?"

It's hard to count with one eye closed, but it's harder to count with the sun burning my cornea, so I did my best. Half the guys were snickering, or at least trying their best not to, while the other half were staring at me incomprehensibly. Not to worry. These were the guys here for the first time. By the next visit they'd be among the snickerers.

"Six?"

"Do you know what today is?"

"Yes."

"Care to tell me?"

"Not particularly."

"Last question: Do manatees talk?"

The snickering became outright laughter, and the second in command knew the interview was over. He poured the coffee for everyone else before lighting a cigarette. Still, I had a question to answer.

"Only during high tides and full moons. Since neither is happening now, the answer must be no."

It was a lie we allowed the other to believe. He believed obviously that them talking at all was a lie, and I figured it'd be best not to disabuse him of that notion, at least for now. He was handed two cups of coffee and passed one over as he slid down next to me. There were plenty of other places he could have sat that would have been more comfortable; as the boss it was certainly his right to demand it. I never knew if he did this for me, him or them.

"How's the wife?"

"She's good, real good." He looked around for spies. "Shit I guess I can tell you. It's not like you talk to people. She's pregnant."

"That's great. Has she told you who the father is?"

"You know I don't have to provide these wake up calls."

"But you enjoy it, and if you didn't we'd never see each other. Besides, you're far more dependable than an alarm clock. Why the hush hush?"

"It's early and she's paranoid."

"Always safe so never sorry. I swear that's going to be on her tombstone."

"She's actually thinking of getting a tattoo that says exactly that."

"Thinking is all she should be doing about it. When it comes to being practically perfect in every way, she makes Mary Poppins look like a common streetwalker, and practically perfect people do not get tattoos."

"I'll tell her you said that. She sends her love."

The only response I had for that was to smile. I closed my eyes and leaned my head back against the bulkhead. The heat from the sun melted into my face. Around me I could hear the sounds of the harbor waking up. The boat rocked on the gentle flow of the tide and bounced atonally against the occasional wake. Feet shuffled now and again, and the crew's radio emitted a low-level continual squawking, letting me know I still had company.

It's considered rude to fall asleep in front of your guests, but the sun must have tapped into the last reservoir of sleep that was in my system. Still I spoke before he did.

"I'm awake. Really, I am."

"Prove it." The voice came from above me, so I guessed he and his crew were getting ready to leave. I decided to show off, so I kept my eyes closed and said:

"Could a sleeping man do this?" With my legs already folded underneath me it was easy to extend them like a spring and rise up to my feet. For a dramatic flourish, I took a long sip of my now lukewarm coffee before I opened my eyes.

He had the look of business about his face, but his eyes smiled as he talked. "Just wanted to be sure we did our job. I'm down starting next Tuesday, so don't be a stranger."

"I'll do my best," but we both knew that my best usually meant staying within my predictable routines. I knew I should make more an effort if she was pregnant, but I wasn't making promises to myself, much less anyone else. As they left I felt more awake than I had, and I knew the last of the cobwebs had been cleaned. In a little bit I would get into my dinghy, head into town and find the corpse that started this story.

Which brought me back to my current dilemma. If all that happened yesterday, what the hell are they doing back on my boat today?

Chapter 13

I've learned a few things over the years that have kept me safe when I really wasn't and alive when other people had different plans for me. Probably the best and most basic one is "Know your surroundings." A lot of other sayings – "Look before you leap," Don't go off halfcocked," "Ears open, mouth shut" – are all subsets of this one simple tenet.

So do you think I listen to myself? Of course not.

In my defense I saw the same Coast Guard boat that had swung by yesterday and simply assumed my nephew was back for another visit. I had long put the conversation with the Chief out of my mind, albeit with a little help. Even if I hadn't, I'm not sure I would have made the connection. That might have come in handy.

I started talking even before I made it to the top of the ladder. "Didn't we do this already yesterday?" The answer was quickly obvious to me. I did it yesterday, but with an entirely different group of Coasties.

"Are you Richard Lockhart?"

"Yes sir."

I felt dumb saying sir to a kid that didn't look old enough to pour me a drink, but the German Shepard who stood at his heel let me know it was definitely in my interest to be on my best behavior.

"We have a warrant to search this vessel and remove any contraband."

"Not that I doubt you, but may I see that?"

He handed it off to me and I took a few minutes to read it

over. From the corner of my eye I could see his crew standing at attention, not a smile among them. They were at least being courteous enough to wait until I was done reading before they started their search, but I could tell this wasn't some form of a practical joke. All the same, I looked the warrant over to be sure I wasn't missing what I wasn't seeing.

"This is just a search warrant."

"Yes."

"No instructions on what to do with me if you find anything."

"No."

"Does that change if your dog here hits the jackpot?"

"No."

"Wow. Must be my lucky day."

"Must be. When we found the hatch locked we were told to stand down and wait for the occupant." I watched as he rearranged the shape of his mouth, making sure I knew his next words were also for the crew's benefit as much as mine. "Our friend here must know somebody special."

"I used to date Elizabeth Taylor, but I don't think she has much pull in something like this."

"Who?"

"That's right. They probably don't let you see lots of movies when you're in training."

"No they don't. We spend too much time making sure we know how to bust people like you, even when we're not supposed to."

He knew someone had him by the short hairs and he didn't like it, but he also knew he had me the same way, and I more than didn't like it. I guess I should be thankful that the Chief was doing this to prove a point and nothing else. Like I said yesterday, this was the Coast Guard's playground, and they had the right to deal with criminals anyway they wanted to. Typically that meant not having to get permission to open a locked hatch and not letting people in possession of drugs go.

That thought did nothing to appease me. In fact, it only made my blood boil more.

Seven crew.

Seven side arms.

One dog.

Twenty seconds, tops. Maybe a gunshot wound. Most definitely a dog bite. Instincts don't go away, but neither do assaults on uniformed officers. I took a deep breath. "Well, like I said, must be my lucky day."

The kid wasn't quite done twisting my nuts. "Another two minutes and we would have stopped waiting." He did his best to make sure I knew what he meant. I did my best not to break his nose.

"Thank heavens I'm a fast swimmer."

"Unlock the hatch and step aside."

I did exactly as I was instructed. I knew that any offer to help would be dismissed without acknowledgement. They would think I was steering them in the wrong direction, or trying to hide something, but it would be useless to do so. That dog was here for a reason and he was looking to earn his pay just like anyone else. Besides, right now that dog was my best friend and probably the smartest one on my boat. He would do exactly his job and only his job, and that was what I needed him to do. I moved away and started brewing a pot of coffee.

A small pot. There would be no sharing today.

As it brewed I watched my newest friend climb down to her dinghy and set off for Miami. She had been moored here for just over six months, and yet had managed to stay out of my sight line all the way until a few nights ago. Travel for her job took care of some of that, but that still left a lot of unaccounted time. Before I retired that wouldn't have bothered me, mostly because I wouldn't have let it happen. I figured when she got back I would find some way to learn about how I'd been missing her all that time. That, and find out what her name is.

Remember, know your surroundings.

I usually didn't care about such things, but that was before I found a dead body in the water, my least favorite boss had moved to my island (and become Chief of police) and the Coast Guard searching my boat all within a twenty-four hour period. You could chalk it all up to coincidences, and maybe that's all it was, but right now I couldn't be sure. At least I had a couple of days to figure out how she fit into it all.

By the time the coffee was ready the dog was losing his mind below deck like, well, like a drug sniffing dog in a room full of drugs. The thought of how his handlers were trying to deal with him while he was freaking out made me chuckle, and nothing looks more suspicious than a person laughing to themselves, so naturally I made sure the one crew man tasked with keeping an eye on me saw my cackle.

See, I don't have a lot of a few drugs. I have a little of a lot of different drugs. At least for a few more minutes. To ensure the quality of what I have means going directly to the source. Hard trips all of them, so I tried to stock up as best I could on each trip. Every drug has a different scent, which is going to elicit a different response from the dog. Then, when he smells the same one again, he runs back and forth between them before the handler gets him off the smell. Think of it as a good old fashioned game of hot and cold.

Intermittently crew members came up with various bags,

bottles and boxes. One guy had the job of trying to inventory all of it. Some of it was pretty obvious to him. I did a good job of labeling stuff, and I don't care how straight edge you are, you will know marijuana when you see it. The rest of the stuff was pretty exotic and I know they hadn't seen it before. I could have told him what all of it was, but I figured they had a chemist back on base. I didn't get in the way of the dog doing the dog's job; why should I get in his way?

The hot coffee helped to cool my blood and I decided to try and make nice with my babysitter.

"Where you from sailor?"

"Tennessee."

"Probably a bit different down here than what you're used to, with the palm trees and such."

"Yes."

I could tell that, as a sailor he didn't want to answer my questions, but as a properly raised southerner who was taught to show respect and be kind he somehow thought that if he didn't his mom would be waiting for him on the base.

"Been down here long?"

"Three months."

"Your friends are probably jealous."

"Probably."

"Do you know Petty Officer Thomas?"

Finally something moved other than his mouth. His eyes popped just for a second, like a busted hand that drew an inside straight. I knew the next words out of his mouth were going to be a lie.

"It's a large base. I haven't met everyone."

I stand corrected. What he said was factually true. And by using four times as many words as he had to answer any of my previous questions, he told me everything I needed to

49

know.

Eventually the dog was done and the crew all came up, prepared to leave. Commander Kid was the last one to come on deck.

"We're finished; unless there is anything else you need to tell us."

"I was at the Kennedy assassination, but I bent over to tie my shoe when it happened, so I missed it all."

He hated me with everything he could, and now that my blood had cooled I was loving it.

"Seriously, ask the babushka lady."

"Last chance."

"For what? You've done all you're allowed to do and you know if you try to do any more, the hot water I soak in will feel like a spa compared to the headhunters cauldron you end up in. Besides, you didn't want my help before."

He gave a sharp nod to his crew and they began to board their boat. "The next time I catch you swimming in the harbor you'll be spending the night with us."

He left without looking back, and I waited without watching them go. Finally I refilled my cup and headed to the hatch.

About a third of the way down I stopped to light a cigarette and do a quick check of where they had been hunting. I saw eight open drawers and cabinets, which was the proper number. I also saw a dozen more compartments that they had missed, lucky thirteen if you throw the engine well in there with them. Some of the hiding spots were just that, hidden, and as for the rest I guess I should just be thankful they didn't open any of the obvious ones that the dog hadn't sniffed out. They would have been well within their normal rights, but that restriction must have been more of what someone special had told them.

I knew exactly who that special someone was, and as soon as I was done with my cigarette, I was going to pay him a visit and give him a piece of my mind.

Chapter 14

"Dick!"

"No. Me Chief, you Dick."

"I am Dick. You ARE a dick!"

"How is the Coast Guard today?"

"You've been a dick before, and you'll be a dick again, but today you have been the dickiest dick ever!"

"I told them to treat you with respect."

"Ron Jeremy looks at you and says 'Wow, what a dick.'"

"I hope they didn't trash your boat."

"You're more of a dick than both Darrens on 'Bewitched' put together!"

"Are you done?"

I thought about it for a moment. "I think. Dick."

He gestured to the chair opposite his desk and I sat like a petulant high schooler who'd been caught defacing the bathroom walls. "So, do we have an arrangement?"

"Can we review on how many levels this is illegal?"

"You want to talk about illegal? Let's start with you tampering with a crime scene."

"What the hell are you talking about?"

"I talked with my officers and they told me that you were the one who cut the body loose and brought it to the surface."

"It's because apparently you've got island cops who are afraid of the water!"

"In fact, they never even saw the body until you brought it to the surface. Sounds like you knew exactly how the body got there."

I don't know how I learned to take manic anger and turn it into cold steel focus. "I don't leave bodies where they can be found. You know that."

"Still, you're probably my best suspect right now. You know the best way to prove your innocence is to find the guilty party."

"By engaging in police activity I'm not legally entitled to do."

"If it makes you feel better I can deputize you."

"That's hardly the point."

"Then what is the point?"

"The point is it's not my responsibility. The point is I wouldn't know where to begin. The point is I don't care. The point is I've never investigated a murder and I don't feel like starting now. The point is I'm retired."

"The point is you work for me. I told you yesterday that I could make your life a living hell. So you lost some drugs. Big deal. Without even seeing the inventory – and I have no intention of seeing it – I know they only found a fraction of what you have. And if not, then maybe you aren't the man for the job after all."

Even though at this point I knew the score and had no intention of walking away, I had to ask. "If I tell you to fuck off and walk out of here, what's your next move going to be? Send them back for the rest of my supply?"

"You know I can do much worse than that. Are you forgetting how far back we go? I know far too many of your secrets. I know just how dirty your hands are."

"My hands aren't nearly as dirty as your soul."

"I merely oversaw the planning of the operations. You were the one who went into the field."

"You think that matters? In Germany, they fried the

guard who worked the gate just as quickly as they did the guy who ran the ovens."

He sat back in his chair and I knew what he was doing. You don't need two people to do "Good cop, Bad cop." Chief was excellent at doing it all on his own. First was the stick, now came the carrot.

"I need someone I can trust, and as big as our differences are I know I can trust you. You talked about my dirty soul. That's right. That's what you don't have. That's why you walked away from me all those years ago, because you didn't have, or probably more accurately weren't lacking, the right stuff to see the job all the way through. That's why I know you will do this, properly. Because the thought of someone doing this to another person, even to someone you barely know and don't much like, drives you crazy. Hell, you'd even want justice if it had been me in the water."

"What I'd want then is a bright red suit to wear to your funeral."

"Maybe, but you'd be there as much as to look for suspects as to dance on my grave. Look at the situation we're in. Even if we weren't headed into the busiest time of the year down here, do you know how many resources I'd have to tie up for this investigation? These guys are good, but they handle murders, not assassinations, and we both know that's what this is."

"We don't know that." But we did and he didn't have to say it. People think that only famous people and heads of states can be assassinated but that's not true. There are lots of little differences between the two, but the big one is this:

Murderers hide the body so no one can find it.

Assassins stage the body so everyone can see it.

There are hundreds of uninhabited islands, thousands of square miles of mangroves and probably a million different animals that all could have helped arrange for disposal. Instead they picked twelve square feet of water under one of the busiest docks on the harbor in front of one of the most popular bars on the island. It'd be the equivalent of a body getting dumped on Times Square.

"Why do you need anyone? A dead body in the harbor? If this isn't what the Coast Guard is here for then what are they doing?"

"You mean besides waking you up and stealing your drugs?"

"Exactly."

"I called them yesterday when you were on the way over. The short answer is we caught him, we get to mount him. But they offered to help if we need it."

"I say we do!"

"Well, they made it clear that until there is solid evidence that he drown or was killed on the water, they want no part of it. As far as they're concerned, he was killed on dry land and dumped in the harbor."

I couldn't believe he was telling me that with a straight face. "He lives on a fucking sail boat in the middle of a fucking mooring field that the Coast fucking Guard is responsible for."

"Yes, well, be that as it may..."

I always hated that phrase, because it meant whoever you were talking to was done, and now it was time to shit or get off the pot.

"Where do I start?"

"First with the coroner, see what he's figured out. If he drowned, you're off the hook."

"Yeah, and if he didn't, then what?"

"Something you're going to love."

"What's that?"

"Knocking on doors."

"Oh c'mon!" I exploded out of my chair. "Do you know why people live on boats? Because they hate people knocking on their doors. They've spent a lifetime shooing encyclopedia salesmen and Jehovah Witnesses off of their porches. They love privacy, hate people and now you want me to be the Avon lady? These people here, they don't shoo. They shoot!"

"You got a better idea?"

"Yeah, get a cop!"

He leaned across the deck. Here comes the stick again.

"Should I send out the Coast Guard back out?"

I'm not going to lie, it was a tempting thought. But this time he would make sure they didn't wait. By the time they were done there'd be nothing left of my boat.

"If I do this, I do this my way, my terms on my time."

"If?"

"I'm still not convinced I wouldn't be better off dragging you through the mud pits with me."

"You're forgetting something. You're retired. Nobody cares what happens to you. I'm still an asset. You're just a liability."

I wished he was just being a dick again, but I knew it was the truth. I never worked for a company that applauded your longevity with them by giving you a gold watch and a pension for life. I was a commodity, and when my cost outweighed my value, I was expendable. Like it or not, I had to make the best of it.

On the plus side, the coroner's got the best air conditioning on the island.

Chapter 15

If I was going to be stuck doing this, I needed to find the positives in it. Going to the coroner's office was one of them. Not because I have a fascination with dead people, and not only because of the great air conditioning, but because it gave me a chance to get back on the water. Most people don't realize that the majority of medical examiner's offices are located where the most people end up dead: the hospital. (Hey, it happens.) Nobody wants to think about it, but they gotta put a morgue where the business is.

The problem with hospitals, from a real estate standpoint, is that they take up a lot of space without generating an equitable amount of tax dollars. The land that they sit on can be used for buildings that are far more profitable than hospitals. Don't believe me? Check with the people who live New York's West Village. Their hospital just got converted into condos.

The added bonus here was that by the time the island got populated enough to warrant a 'modern hospital' all of the desirable real estate was taken up. Best spot they could find was on the next island up the road. It would have been a hell of a long walk, but it was a lovely day for a cruise.

The drawback was that even though it was an island hospital, the ambulances still arrived on wheels. I took a calculated guess where the best spot to tie off would be, and settled for a commercial dock at the local residential marina. Without a mooring field nearby they didn't get a lot of strangers coming up, but the old guy whose job it was to keep out the undesirables was placated by a twenty dollar bill.

Asking questions is a good way to attract attention, but so is wandering around aimlessly. The trick is to act like you've been there before and someone is expecting you. I had no idea where the morgue might be, but I knew it had to be somewhere people could get to with minimal hassle and yet not be right next to the gift shop. Finding a corridor at the other end of the elevator bank lined with laboratories seemed like a good shot. Sure enough, as far as it could be from everything else and still have the same mailing address, there it was.

Inside it was like any other doctor's office. I rang the bell and waited, remarking to myself on how tastefully decorated the waiting room was considering how rarely it was probably used. There was even a current issue of Saltwater Angler that I was thumbing through when a voice broke my concentration.

"Can I help you?"

"Yeah I'm here to see the coroner." I've never met him professionally but had seen him enough times out and about to recognize that this wasn't his voice, so I kept reading the article I was on.

"Yes, can I help you?"

I looked up and sure enough I was right.

"Yeah you can help me by getting the coroner."

"We prefer the term medical examiner."

"I'm sure that's a big comfort to your corpses. But, fine, I'll play your game. Yeah you can help me by getting the medical examiner."

"Yes, can I help you?"

I'll grant you that you probably have to have a sense of

humor when the majority of time is spent surrounded by dead people. I would just expect it to be a little more along the lines of gallows humor and less like that of a six year old. This was not the week to be fucking with me.

"I need the medical examiner."

"I am the medical examiner."

"No, you may be *A* medical examiner, but I need *THE* medical examiner, the guy who works here and not some intern on a field trip."

He laughed in a genuine way that broke the tension. "You must have been expecting Dr. Santacrose. Called out sick a couple of days ago and they sent me down from Miami. I'm Dr. Cornelius White."

His manner and handshake was so disarming it almost made me happy to meet him. "Tough name. I hope the ancestor you're named for was a nice guy."

"Not if the police reports were true."

And a decent sense of humor after all. Maybe this wouldn't be the shit show I expected. "I'm Dick Lockhart."

"Just got off the horn with the Chief about you. Come on back." He held the door and I followed him through the sterile hallway.

"Must be a nice break to get sent down here for a change."

"In more ways than one. Barely had time to pack a bag, but having been unemployed for so long I'm not complaining."

"Unemployed?"

"Or so I thought. I applied with Miami-Dade County a few months back. Went through all the interviews and pre-employment screenings, only to be told they had nothing available at the time. Said they'd call me if something came up."

"Something certainly did."

"You're telling me. I've been trying to think of all the examples we went through when I was studying, and I'm pretty sure this guy takes the cake."

You know what you never see on television? What a real autopsy looks like. The only part of Scooter that was still Scooter was his face. Pretty much everything below his chin was sliced open and spread out. I'm not going to lie; it was the best he's looked in a long time.

"You know what my sixty-four thousand dollar question is."

"Huh?"

Right, still wet behind his ears. Come to think of it, I don't think I ever saw that game show, just knew the slogan. "What did he die from?"

"All sorts of things. Starting here." He pointed to the crook of the elbow. There was the tell-tale sign of a needle. "The same thing on the other arm. One plunge each side. Hit the vein on this side, missed it horribly on the other."

I walked around and could see some pretty serious discoloration beneath the skin. "What was it and how much did they use?"

"The how much is hard to figure out because of their lack of accuracy. Best guess is a couple of liters."

"Of?"

"Antifreeze."

I didn't know that my subconscious had started a list of all the possibilities. Antifreeze apparently had not been on the list and the omission must have registered on my face.

"That's right. Poisoned, not drowned."

I pointed to some unusual bruising around his mouth. "Is that a reaction to the antifreeze?"

He laughed. I guess he did have a dark streak of humor

after all. "Oh no. That's from where they shoved the pipe down his esophagus."

"Why the hell would they do that?"

He had reached behind to the adjoining table and struggled with a bag. "So they could fill him with this."

The bag fell heavy on the table next to Scooter, and I could hear what sounded a collection of bearings or marbles resettling. I looked at him but he said nothing, just stared at the bag, so I took that as an invitation and stuck my hand in. They felt like rocks, but metallic. I grabbed a handful so I could look at them.

"Fishing weights."

"Fifty pounds of them. All in his stomach."

"I don't get it. They had him tied down. If they wanted him sunk, just tie him closer to the seabed."

"My guess is they didn't want him that low in the water."

"Low enough to be partially hidden, but floating just enough to be seen."

"Precisely."

If there was any doubt still left it was washed away. Somebody wanted Scooter dead with a message. I knew how. Now I needed to know when.

"Well," he said as he covered the body and led us to a sink to wash up, "that's where it gets even weirder, if you can believe that. Based on rigor mortis and water saturation I'd say it was right around seventy-two hours before he was found. He was alive but probably not by much when they pumped the weight into him."

I can't believe I was going to say this, but I did. "That doesn't sound too weird."

"Except that he doesn't show the damage you'd expect from being where you found him for seventy-two hours. Looking at how he's been picked at by the tarpon, and not nibbled on by any night feeders, it looks like someone might have slipped him under the dock just around dawn yesterday morning."

If that were the case I'd have to check with my nephew to see if him and his crew had been out early enough to have seen anything suspicious. For now though it was probably in my best interest to avoid the Coast Guard for a while.

"They killed him and sat on him for three days?"

"Pretty much. They poisoned him, pumped him full of ballast, dropped him in the drink for a couple of days and then, for whatever reason, decided he needed a new spot to call home." He grabbed some towels and turned off the water. "Speaking of sitting on him, has he got anyone to claim him?"

"Are you kidding? People around here are lining up to spit on him. He's going to a pauper's grave more likely than not." I thought about it, and realized my final spot would probably be right next to his. "Thanks for the nickel tour. I can't imagine I'm going to need anything else, but if I do."

"You know where to find me."

We walked out in silence and I was almost out the door when it dawned on me. "What are you going to do with the fishing weights?"

"For now keep them with the body. Eventually they'll be classified as evidence, but I'm still running some more tests. I figure on a case this messed up it pays to be extra careful. Once I can determine they were not instrumental in his death, they become property to be claimed by his next of kin. Why? You want them?"

I laughed. "Nah, I already have enough ways to frustrate myself while wasting time. Fishing's a hobby I don't need."

I stepped out of the hospital, slid on my sunglasses and walked back to the dock. The old man was snoozing when I pushed off. I was halfway home before I realized my fingerprints were now all over what might be evidence.

Chapter 16

I don't want you to think that there is only one place on the island to get coffee. There are several, and as for which one's the best, that is all a matter of opinion and what it is you're looking for. Some people need to make sure it's rich and flavorful, and that includes the whole subset of people down here who will only drink Cuban coffee. Other people use coffee the way many people use their happy hour cocktail, as a way to meet up with friends and talk. I use coffee to drink, so as far as I'm concerned the best cup is the closest one.

Candy watched me with a slightly concerned look on her face as I helped myself. "You realize this is the second day in a row you've been here before noon."

"Maybe I'm changing my ways."

"The day you become a morning person is the day I take my vows and join my nunnery."

"You should start practicing your rosary. I've already been to Stock Island and back."

"What could possibly be so important this early in the day?"

I just shrugged. "I had work to do."

"You're retired. You're not supposed to work."

She was already on her way to other customers so I just muttered to myself. "Funny, I thought the same thing. Guess we're both wrong."

I took a seat at the corner of the bar and just tried to clear my head a little. I had two issues confusing me, and Scooter was only one of them.

The Chief knows me, and I mean well. He knows things about me I've never told anyone because he was there when they happened and responsible for arranging them. Which made his presence here as the Chief of police all the more mysterious. The only explanation is because someone in the fed who gets appointed and not elected said so. Remember what I said about coincidence? I couldn't accept that as being the reason he shows up for the job right in the middle of my seven day "vacation." And then a dead body shows up in my neck of the woods and he makes me responsible for it. For all the skills and experience he knows I have, being a murder-solving cop isn't one of them. But if he wasn't here to keep tabs on me, then why put me on his leash? Having a mysterious dead body is a good way to do that. I'm not saying he would have Scooter killed to fill a need.

But I'm also not saying he wouldn't.

My concentration was broken by the shuffling of familiar feet on what constitutes the floor. My day was definitely starting to brighten up.

"How are you Mike?"

"Still pissing in a toilet and not in my pants, so I must be okay." He laughed at his own joke. "How's life by you Tricky? Did you have a good vacation?"

"Just like everyone else's. It was great right up until the last day."

Candy set Mike's G-n-T in front of him and told him how much.

Forty-two fifty.

Trust me, your drink will be cheaper.

Up until yesterday I had enjoyed a pretty steady life of routine, but I had nothing on Mike. Every day it's the same thing. He gets here just before the music starts and spends the day listening, drinking, reading, eating and, his favorite, passionately meeting new people. He's gotta be the most popular person on most people's vacations. The only thing he does more than talk to strangers is smoke his pipe, hence the name: Mike the Pipe.

He already had it set up for the first smoke of the day as he pulled money from his wallet. If Mike has a fault – and pretty much everyone will tell you that he doesn't – it's that when he is done for the night, he is done right then. He just slips away with no goodbye and no paying his tab. At first it was a pretty serious issue, and can still be a snafu when breaking in a new bartender, but now they know he'll be back every day. So they run him a separate tab and he pays it the following morning.

"I'd like to sponsor my friend Tricky to a drink too, as soon as he's done with that silly coffee," he said as he handed Candy the money. That's mostly how his tabs got as big as they did, his generosity, and I'm sure he probably had more drinks bought for him than he bought in a night.

"Thanks Mike, but I have work to do today."

"You're retired. You're not supposed to work."

Since it was the second time someone said that to me today, I decided to take it as a sign. I chugged what was left of my coffee while thinking I could always work tomorrow. Besides, it's not like Scooter is going to get anymore dead.

"Fuck it, I'll have a beer."

Mike and I toasted and he settled in next to me. "I'm actually glad you're here. I got something to talk about and I figure you're about the perfect guy to talk to."

"Yeah? How you go about figuring that?"

"Because your balls are bigger than your brain, but you're not so dumb to forget what part of your anatomy is for thinking with."

"Wow. That might be the most unique compliment I've ever gotten. What's on your mind?"

He leaned in close. "Did'ja hear about Scooter?"

I nodded my head while taking a sip of my beer, suddenly no longer liking the taste of it. Mike took a look around to make sure nobody was listening.

"I'm the guy who killed him."

So much for me not working today.

Chapter 17

"About six years ago Scooter comes up to me here at the bar. He was even less social back then, if you can believe it, than he is now, was now. Come in once a week maybe, sit by himself, have a few drinks, bother nobody, go home.

"Well he comes up to me and tells me he's in a spot, could I help him out? Obviously I don't know him well but I know him well enough, you know? I ask him how much, and he gives me a figure. It's a lot. I mean a lot to even ask for among friends, but a lot a lot to drop on one bar regular to another. I tell him that, tell him I gotta think about it, and even if it's yes it'll take me a few days to get the cash. He thanks me, says no hurry, and goes back to his corner.

"So I think about it. My first thought is how tight can the spot be, if there's no hurry? But I know we all get into our own jams in our own ways, and if he has time then so be it. Then I think am I being dumb? Way I see it the worst case scenario is he takes it and skips town, never to be seen again. Sure I'd be pissed, but here's the thing Dick.

"If I needed it for just that reason and I knew someone could give it to me and not miss it, I'd want them to. Like I said, it was a lot of money, but the truth is I got a lot more and wouldn't miss it if walked out of my life. I'm lucky that way. So I go to the bank, get the cash, and sure enough next day he's here waiting for me. It's like he could smell it.

"He takes it, thanks me profusely, tells me he'll pay me back as soon as he can, and takes off for his boat. A week goes by, I don't see him. His boat is still there, but there are plenty of other ways to get off the island. I don't want to ask around because I don't like people knowing my business – you're an exception Dick, but you already know that – and I'm ready to chalk it up to experience when I hear him one night. Or at least I think I do.

"In all the time I've known him I've never heard him laugh. But this night I hear a guy laughing the way I imagine he would sound. He's down at the jukebox end of the bar with these guys, out of towners all, and they're having a time. What's more, he looks different. I mean same clothes, same hair, same everything, but different, you know? Younger, maybe. Whatever. I figure it's on account of him laughing.

"This goes on for four or five days. Same guys, same place, same laughter. I figure this is his spot, you know? He needed to drop a little in order to make a lot, we've all been there. I don't want to interfere so I say nothing and figure he'll fill me in after they leave town.

"A couple of days of nothing and then one night he's back in here by himself. Doesn't thank me for the money, doesn't say a word to me, doesn't even acknowledge my presence. Okay fine, maybe his deal got burned, what do I know? But then he starts talking up strangers, buying them drinks, being the life of the party. Every night this goes on, new people, new good times.

"Maybe I'm petty, maybe I just sound that way. You know me, I don't begrudge anyone a good time, and I'm always buying drinks for people, but there was something about him. It was like he was doing it to spite me. And the fact that he's doing it with my money is the salt in the wound. So finally I think 'Fuck it.' I decide I'm gonna say something. Least he can do is buy me a drink with my money.

"I head down to his end of the bar, work my way into the circle, even start laughing a little to fit in, and finally say something like 'Hey Scooter, looks like you're having a grand time.'

"He stops laughing like someone slit his throat. The tourons around him don't notice, they keep carrying on, but he clams up and looks at me, cold dead stare.

"'Can I help you old man?' he says, and he drags it out so now they do notice. They all turn and look. That's the moment I realize what an unrepentant asshole he is. So I just say 'Yeah, how about you return that money you owe me?' He just looks at me, doesn't say a word. Now it's deadly silent in this circle, everybody's waiting for him, and you know what he does? He laughs. He laughs louder than ever. All of his new found friends laugh with him, and somehow he manages to move the circle so just like that I'm on the outside.

"I don't know why, but I've never felt more humiliated in my life. I go back to my stool and just try to forget the whole thing, but you know what he starts doing then? Anytime he comes in here and sees me, he makes a point of pointing me out to whoever he is with. He would say something to them, and they would all laugh. That was too much. I almost stopped coming in here, but the bartenders convinced me to stay. One of them or more must have said something to him, because he quickly slid back to his antisocial ways before disappearing for a while, and I put the whole thing behind me.

"Last Friday night, after I got home, I hear him on my porch. I hadn't seen him in months, but there he is, drunk as all get out and laughing at me. Something happens and I snap. I grab one of the plants on the porch and just pop him on the head. I didn't think I hit him that hard, but I must have made a love connection because he was done. I don't mean out. I mean done.

"I panic and drag him inside, trying to figure out what to do. Finally, when it's late enough for the drunks to be home but still too early for the fisherman to be getting ready for the day, I drag him out back and fold him into the basket on the back of my trike. I try to stage him so if anyone glances, in the dimness it'll look like one drunken friend giving another one a ride home. I figure if I can dump him in the water down here, people will think he slipped trying to get into his dinghy. Luckily nobody was around so I slid him in the water and hurried back home. I cleaned up the porch, threw out the busted plant, and up until today nobody was the wiser.

"I'm not sorry I did it Dick, and I'm not even sorry he's dead."

Terry

Chapter 18

I wish I could say that's exactly how the story went. Thing is, Mike is old and sociable. What just took you ten, maybe fifteen minutes to read took him over an hour to tell me. People come up to him and say hi, he's gotta talk to them, strangers he wants to meet, asking me "where was I?" after every time they left. Don't get me wrong. It's not like I was in danger of being late to have tea with the Queen. I had all afternoon to waste listening to stories, and Mike's a great guy to keep company with. It was just hard to sit through it all when I knew from the start that it was going to be very entertaining even though, no matter how much of it was true, it was all going to end up as a lie.

"Hell of a story Mike. Sure wish I could believe it." He shot me a look as he lit his pipe and I continued. "Actually that's not all true. There are parts of it I wish I could believe, and parts of it I wish I couldn't. Problem is, the parts I don't want to believe are most likely the truth, and the parts I wish I could believe I know I can't."

It's a delicate thing, calling a man a liar, especially when it's someone you respect. It's a far more delicate thing when you can't explain how you know it's a lie.

"Oh really. And which part is it that you can't believe?"

"C'mon Mike. You know which part."

"You know how much that shitty son of a bitch was into me for?" Mike's face grew red, and this was easily the angriest I've ever seen him.

"I know Mike, and if I were you I'd be pissed too."

"Damn right you would be."

"And if he were to die I wouldn't be losing any sleep over it."

"Not a wink."

"But Mike."

"But what? You gonna to tell me I'm not capable of such a thing?"

I almost was. Almost, but I knew better. You hear people all the time expressing shock, outrage, disbelief when a relative is arrested or a neighbor is convicted of some heinous crime. They all say the same thing. "He never seemed capable of doing something like that." Let me tell you, I have seen every kind of person in every kind of situation, and there is no such thing as a person not being capable of anything. There's darkness in all of us. It may take more for some than others, but everyone can get there if they are pushed to it. After a while, the only thing that surprised me about what I saw people do was that none of it surprised me anymore.

Up until this point, I thought Mike might be the exception to that rule. Polite, generous, kind, disarming, the last person you would certainly expect. Seeing him now, seeing that hurt, that defeated pride and that seething anger, I could tell now how badly he wanted Scooter dead. I could almost believe that he did do it.

Except for, of course, you know, all of the wrong facts.

Still, if I said "No Mike, you're not capable of that" I would be stinging his pride just about as much as Scooter had when he laughed at him. I also couldn't say "No Mike, because I know exactly how he was killed" because then I would be in a place I didn't want to be, even if I felt like the ground was shifting me there anyway. So now I'm back to the point where I need to tell Mike he's a liar without actually calling him a liar. Seemed like the perfect time to drop my cigarettes on the ground.

"Ah clumsy me. Can you grab those for me Mike?"

And this is how I know that if there is an exception to the "capable" rule Mike is it. He doesn't tell me to piss off and pick up my own cigarettes. He doesn't look me in the eye and say "You know what? You got me. Of course I'm too old and worn down to bend over that far, much less drag a body into the water." Nope. He just does what comes naturally to a person who is as genuinely kind and nice as Mike. He puts down his pipe, he slides off his stool and, using it for support, he leans over slowly, working his way down to get my cigarettes.

It takes almost a minute before he's back to being vertical, and now he knows.

"I'm sorry Mike. If it helps I can see about somehow getting your money back."

He shakes his head. "I gave up on that money a long time ago. I gave up on a lot of things a long time ago. I even thought I had given up on him, but there he was, showing back up."

I didn't understand what he was getting at with that last statement, but I figured it had something to do with Scooter coming back to taunt him, or asking for more help, or just the distraught ramblings of an old man so I let it go while I lit a cigarette.

"If I was younger, when I was younger, I could have and would have, you know?"

"I do. But be glad that you didn't do it now. Prison can be hell on an old man."

He laughed. "Maybe they'd go easy on me, seeing as how I might remind them of their grandfather."

I was glad he was back to being Mike the Pipe, and I

laughed with him. Then he did it again, said something else that made no sense.

"Should have done it when I was younger, when I had the chance. But I didn't, and then he was gone."

But before I could ask him what he meant by that, a pretty girl walked by and Mike had someone new to talk to.

Chapter 19

After I disabused Mike of the notion that he was the murderer and bought him a drink to make up for calling him a liar, it would have been nice to say that I felt the call and responsibility of my duty and began the next step of my investigation in earnest. That didn't happen. I sat and listened to the music a little while longer before deciding to head downtown. I may have only had a couple of blocks to go, but that walk can take all afternoon.

The best thing about living in a small island town is that you get to know the locals real fast. This can be a bad thing if you're a jerk, because then you have nobody to talk to but the tourists. It can also be a problem if you happen to think that somebody's a jerk, but the two of you like to hang out at the same places, because then you're gonna be stuck with them. Plus you have to be willing to talk about the same shit day after day. Not much happens down here, so there isn't that much to discuss. And if you don't like everyone knowing your business, or you knowing everyone else's, it's not such a good thing either.

Did I say the best thing? Let's try this:

One of the good things about living in a small island town is that you get to know the locals real fast. As far as I know, most people don't think I'm a jerk, I've been lucky enough not to meet too many, I love making small talk at this point in my life, and living on a boat keeps me off of most people's radar.

That two block walk included stopping a dozen times. I

know people who are tending bar, run into familiar faces on the street, see people I know having lunch and join them for a bite, pop in on people working the shops and galleries, and next thing you know three hours have gone by and I'm only now making it to Duval Street.

I may be big on small talk but I'm not a fan of big crowds. Duval Street might be one of the most famous streets in the world when it comes to having a good time, but it's too much like amateur hour for me. I'm sure I knew a few people who were working, but those who know me know me well enough to not expect me until the coast is clear.

I pushed through the crowds and ducked down the alley that the Pelican Deck was on. For better or worse being only a couple hundred feet from the craziness made them invisible to some people. Cruisers usually stumble down the gangplank with a strict itinerary and a stop watch, and come hell or high water they are going to do everything on that list and only what is on that list. God forbid they get back late and miss the latest slopping of the trough. Because of that, afternoons could be hit or miss, but Tony Roberts, a local musician with a loyal and large following, was on stage. I snuck into a corner stool and Yeddie dropped me my beer with a nod. Somebody was missing from behind the bar and he was doing all he could to keep up.

By now I know what you're thinking: "DUDE! There's a dead body and all you can do is go drink at your favorite bars. Don't you care?" I won't answer that question, because I know you won't like what my answer would be, so I'll just move on to your next question: when am I going to start interviewing witnesses?

A guy gets murdered the way Scooter did, witnesses are going to be the last thing I find, because there weren't any then or there aren't any now. Best I'm going to do by talking

Terry

to people now is hear stories about strange things they saw. And I'm not just talking about boats they never saw before and people they didn't recognize. I mean every strange thing they ever experienced, or thought they experienced, or heard about somebody experiencing, or wished they would experience, and how it all suddenly had something to do with the murder of a person they don't care about.

(For the record, a talking manatee does not qualify as a strange thing. Talking manatees, plural, maybe, but not one renegade manatee.)

Besides, if you've been paying attention then you've noticed how people are falling all over themselves to take credit for it. I'll go out looking for clues and end up coming back with a book full of confessions. We'd have to have some sort of round robin tournament just to thin the crowd down to a top five.

The place I need to start with is his boat. I know it ain't going anywhere, but trust me, that is only one of the reasons I'm avoiding it.

Yeddie came back with another beer and a shot. I raised it to toast to him but he was already halfway back down the bar throwing the empty shot glass away. I slid a twenty dollar bill under my empty beer and surrendered my stool. The sky was looking good and the timing was just about right. I was going to slip out the backway and make myself to the sunset, but as I crossed the patio by the back bar I saw a familiar face that might be able to explain what's been bugging me all day.

"Smiling John." I popped off a crisp left handed salute and waited until he did the same. After thirty years in the Coast Guard he retired to become an admiral in the Conch Republic Navy. They salute with their left hand for the practical reason that there's usually a drink in the right.

"Mr. Lockhart, always a pleasure. May I buy you a drink?"

"Would love to but I'm off to the sunset. I do have a question I hope you can clear up for me."

"Too late, you can take it with you." Being an admiral had pull, and the bartender was there with two drinks immediately. "Ask away."

"How many different crews does the Guard have patrolling the mooring field?"

"In a word, none. At least not on a regular basis. Unless they're going out for inspections or to answer a distress call, they figure their going back and forth is presence enough."

"So it wouldn't be uncommon to be visited by two different crews in two consecutive days?"

"No that would be very uncommon. It would mean that you were a very bad boy and didn't follow instructions the first time."

"The first visit was social, the second all business." While he thought, I added "The guy who made the social call is still on duty until next week."

"And the business call, they came for you, or were just out taking a survey?"

"It was all about me."

He thought a bit more before rendering his judgment. "It isn't the strangest thing to happen. Somebody called, lodged a complaint, or they had a suspicion,"

"Or search warrant."

Now his ears perked up. "A warrant, eh? Well, then my guess is that someone knows there was a social call the day before, and maybe that person wouldn't be the best candidate for the job."

I never thought about how that might jeopardize my nephew's career, mostly because I never planned on being boarded by the Coast Guard.

"Could something like that get him in trouble?"

"Could, but most likely not. Whether you're in uniform or not, sailors all have a way of becoming friends. If anything, they probably didn't want him in an awkward situation."

That set my mind more at ease, but as I thanked him I made a mental note that it was more important than ever to make sure I swung by for a visit. Unanswered questions were starting to pile up, and I wasn't getting any happier about it.

Chapter 20

People always talk about how they never do anything that is famous or popular where they live until their friends come to visit. Instead, they just take it for granted. Down here, with a list of things to see and do and everything else, the top of the food chain is the sunset. I haven't missed one yet since I've been retired, and no matter where you are on the island, you see almost everyone try to stop what they're doing and enjoy it. There are plenty of bars, restaurants, beaches, hotels and boats to watch it from, but there is one place they say made the Key West sunset famous. Kids may run off to join the circus, but for those who find the circus boring, they run off from that and come to Mallory Square.

I got a mojito and a bag of popcorn as I stepped into the square and began to navigate my way through the growing crowd. I still get a kick out of watching the performers even if I have most of their spiel memorized and have seen their act a hundred times. Part of the pleasure comes not so much from watching them, but watching the people see them for the first time and witnessing their reactions. There's no replacing the feeling you get when you see something being performed live, especially if it's something that doesn't happen that often – juggling, sword swallowing, even a trained cat act. The acts go on for about an hour before the big finale of the sun, and it always makes for a great viewing experience.

You still get some kids that are too cool for anything their parents want them to do. They have their head down, ear piece in, eyes glued to whatever it is they think is more important. I feel bad for the parents who spend their entire vacation, begging, pleading and fighting with their kids. They ruin their own vacation trying to give their kid memories they just aren't interested in. But I don't feel too bad. After all, who gave the kid that distraction in the first place?

There was a family like that as I got close to the edge and the sun was finally starting to set. The mother was trying to arrange a family portrait and had found a willing sucker to take the picture. One of the kids couldn't be bothered to look at the camera. Finally he put the game down long enough to offer a disgusted expression and the picture was taken. He went right back to what he was doing and didn't even notice the sun had set until he heard the applause.

"What's the big deal? The sun sets every day. Oooooh, so special! Who cares? It'll set again tomorrow."

That's right kid. It'll just keep setting day after day. Until one day it sets and you're no longer around to take it for granted.

Chapter 21

I was glad that Candy was not working in the morning because I didn't want to face her seeing me for a third morning in a row. The rational part of me knew that she would make some snarky comment, probably even pretend to faint from the shock, but at this point in the game I was starting to also put a little trust in the less rational side of my brain.

There's a rule of 3, and it is used by scientists and comics alike. Think of all the jokes you've heard that involve three people. I don't know why a black guy and a white guy walking into a bar isn't funny, and a black guy, a white and a Latino guy is, but there ain't too many jokes featuring a duo. Scientists look at it a little more, you know, scientifically: if something happens once it's an aberration. If it happens twice it's a coincidence. Third time is a charm; it becomes as far as their concerned a statistical fact. Seeing me here three days in a row for my cup of coffee might make her start to cut through the bullshit and want to know what really was going on, and that was a conversation I just didn't want to have.

The walk through old town cleared my head and gave me some measure of peace. I tried to think of the last time I had seen my "niece". I had really embraced the essence of retirement where you do not keep track of time, and this worked on weeks and months just as effectively as it did on hours and days. I was taking a chance just showing up, but that was the burden of having no phone. And if she wasn't there, at least I would have gotten some exercise since my impromptu swim yesterday morning.

It was my lucky day however. The cautious look most people wear when they open the door melted the second she saw me, and threw the door wide to give me a hug.

"Uncle Dickie!" The name was cute when she was four and five years old. Now that she wasn't, it just made me feel foolish. Still, old habits die hard and I know I had to cut her some slack. Part of the reason I stayed away from seeing her was guilt I put on myself. I know I was no more responsible for her father dying than anyone else who worked with us was, including himself, but I was also the only person she still saw from the old days. Watching how tough it had been for her to grow up without a father always made me wish I could have done more.

"Hey Jessie, how you doing?" She stepped back and led me into the apartment. Cozy like so many others on the island, it made up for it by having a large back deck that overlooked the common pool area. "Johnny warn you I might be stopping by?"

"He mentioned he invited you, but we both know what the invite means."

See? Was I reading too much into it, or was she trying to be a bit snarky? I had to remind myself that if she had something on her mind, in the right company she was not afraid to say it, and I definitely qualified as that kind of company.

"Well, you know how it is. You get settled into a routine, habits become harder to break, next thing you know, you're wondering where the time has gone."

"Mm-hmm." She gave me a once over, trying to read the tea leaves and figure out why today was special. "Still drinking Barnacle Bob's shit coffee and telling yourself that it's breakfast"

"Always, unless you got something tastier."

"I will in five minutes. Have a seat."

"Thanks, but do you mind if we go out back? Unless it's too uncomfortable for you?"

"Not this time of year. Weather's still everything I hope for." She got about halfway in the kitchen before she realized why I was asking, and kept talking as she put the coffee on. "Johnny told you, I guess?"

"Yeah, he figured the secret was safe with me."

"I would imagine it is. I rarely see any of your posts show up on my Facebook feed, and I don't think I'm following you on Twitter." She poked her head back out of the kitchen. "You do know what those are, don't you?"

"Modern equivalent of carrier pigeons and smoke signals, if I'm not mistaken."

She laughed and returned to her task at hand. "I don't get you, Uncle Dick. It's a modern world; you should feel free to join it one of these days."

"Thanks but I've seen more than enough of it." I've seen her maybe a handful of times since she turned eighteen, but I still knew her body language well enough to know my last words tensed her up, and I knew why. I saw too much of the world, and her father had never seen enough. "Mind if I step out back for a cigarette?"

"Make yourself comfortable." Her voice had become cold and flat. "I'll be right out with the coffee."

I didn't really want the cigarette as much as I needed the excuse to leave, but I knew I had to make appearances so I lit one as I settled into a chair with a view of the pool. I felt a little bad for Johnny when he met Jessie. I don't think he really knew what he was getting himself into. I knew that she loved him very much and was deeply devoted to him, but I also knew she carried a lot of pain and anger, both of which had made her sharp. That was the problem. I had to try and get some information from her without her knowing I was going fishing. Too bad she already knew most of my lures.

Chapter 22

"How far along are you?"

"Only a few months. It's going to be a bitch when the summer really kicks in and I'm as fat as a whale. I'm excited to be pregnant, but I wish we could have timed it a little better." I suggested that maybe he'd be able to arrange a transfer before then but she just waved me off. "Most places we could end up still have hot summers, and those that don't have ice cold winters. Given the two, I'd rather sweat than freeze." Almost immediately a smile came to her face.

"What?"

"Some poem we had to learn in high school. Something about how the world would end, either fire or ice. I guess the poet liked warm weather too, because I think he chose fire."

"Robert Frost."

"Ironic name for a guy who writes a poem about the weather, don't you think?"

"Well, not all of his poems are meteorological."

"I should hope not. Probably a pretty limited field." She laughed at her own joke, and I could finally get around to why I had come here.

"Do you two talk about him transferring out of here?"

"Now and then. Key West is definitely fun for two people, but I'm not sure if it's where we want to raise a family."

"Why not? Lots of other people do."

"Well, it may not be up to us. They may want to keep him here for the foreseeable future."

"Has there been talk about a promotion?"

"I don't know about that, but I do know that they've selected him to go on some special mission."

"That's cool. When does that start?"

"It started yesterday morning."

Meaning part of the reason he wasn't the one to search my ship was because he wasn't around to do it. "Huh. Surprised he didn't mention anything about it when I saw him the other morning."

"How could he have? He only found out about it yesterday."

She was making it seem like she thought this was a natural occurrence, but I knew that what was racing through her mind as she cleared the coffee mugs was not the protocol the Coast Guard followed when deploying sailors on missions. When she didn't come back out after a few moments, I went in to find her standing over the kitchen sink trying not to cry.

"He's not doing anything you don't want him to do."

She turned, full of venom and fear. "How do you know that? And if you did, would you tell me anyway?"

"Yes. I would."

"Oh bullshit Dick. You wouldn't and you know it. You, my dad, all of you crazy assholes were all the same: loyalty to your job, secrecy about your job, no matter what it cost."

I stepped in to reassure her, not confident she wouldn't swing out at me if I got to close. "I wouldn't do that to you. I would tell you, because I wouldn't want to risk you going through this twice."

"Then why the secrecy?" She pushed through me and went into the living room.

"Tell me what happened." I sat opposite her on the sofa, making sure I wasn't directly in her line of vision so she would feel relaxed enough to talk.

"Yesterday morning, about an hour before his alarm goes off, he gets a phone call. They must have been urgent to talk to him because they only let it ring three times, like they didn't want to risk it going to voice mail. Immediately it rings again, but by then we're both awake. A twenty second call turned into ten minutes later he's heading out the door, telling me he loves me and he'll talk to me when he can." Her jaw was set so hard her veins were starting to show, but she was fighting the urge to cry with all the strength she had. She pushed it down and fixed me with a steely eye. "So tell me. One day he sees you, the next day he's gone and the following day you come waltzing through my door. Tell me what's going on."

There's a fine line between choosing your words carefully so you make your point clearly and taking too long so that people think you're lying. I had to make sure I stayed on that right side of the line. "I can start by telling you what's not happening. He's not following in your father's footsteps."

"You sure about that?"

"Completely. If he were, you'd be one of the last to know, because nothing would appear out of the ordinary until it was too late to turn back?"

"Is that how it was for you? Is that" and the fight she was waging with her tears started to slip a little, "what would have eventually happened with my dad?"

"Yes, to both of those questions. When your dad, when that happened, everything was still so new, none of us knew the commitment it would eventually take. Some left after that, but for those that stayed..."

"It cost you everything."

"Something like that, yeah. But the important thing with Johnny is that's not what's going on. Besides," I didn't quite know how to say what I had to, not after just invoked the memory of her father, but I thought it would help bolster my argument, and I knew it would help to break the tension, "Johnny, he's a nice guy, but that's just it. He's waaay too nice to ever do what we'd been doing."

A smile cracked onto her face. "You mean he's not a dick like you are."

I leaned back in the chair. "Well, nobody's that kind of a dick, but yeah, he's not qualified, and that is a very good thing."

"Can you find out for me what is going on? Maybe ask around the base?"

"Well, that's a problem these days. I'm not sure how welcome I am around there. Had a little run in with one of the boys in charge, and it's probably best I don't show my face until that cools over."

She got the serious look on her face again. "Do you think it might be related?"

"Meaning do you think I got him in trouble?" Of course I was thinking that right now, but there was no way in hell I was going to say that. "Purely unrelated. And it's not a big deal. I've got a friend, retired, he can give me at least some general answers. I may not be able to track down exact coordinates, but I'll at least let you know when he'll be back to hang his laundry."

That took a load of pressure off of her, but it left me in a tighter spot than when I first got here. With Johnny gone I wouldn't be able to ask him if he saw anything funny in the harbor Monday morning. Good thing Jessie was here to tighten the vice for me another click.

"Thanks Uncle Dick," she smiled and stood, letting me know that she expected me to start getting answers now. "I wasn't worried at first really. I thought it had something to do with the early phone call he'd gotten the morning before."

"Oh yeah? What was that one about?"

"They needed him in the harbor right away, before sunrise, to take care of something important."

Terry

Chapter 23

I sat her back down in the chair. I would gladly start getting answers for her in a minute, but I needed to get some from her. "What time was this phone call exactly?"

"I'd have to say 4:30 or so. Same thing, they called for a few rings, hung up and called right back. It was just as short as the conversation he had the next day, but after this one he seemed completely relaxed. He took his time making coffee, showering, like it was another typical morning."

"When did he tell you what the phone call had been about?"

"When I finally said 'What the fuck?' I couldn't figure out why they had called him so early if he could be so nonchalant about getting down there."

People's memories are never as good as you want them to be, especially when recalling a pre-dawn conversation, but I needed her to be as accurate as possible. "What exactly did he tell you?"

"Just that there was something going on in the harbor they needed him for right away. So I said if they're calling you in, then shouldn't you be moving a little faster? But he just laughed, and said it wasn't as big a deal as they were making it out to be. He almost made it seem like it was something he'd been expecting, he was that relaxed."

"Do you remember what time he left?"

"Probably about an hour after the phone call."

5:30. That would give him plenty of time to get on base, get his crew – or not – and get out on the boat, all before sunrise. The same time that somebody was tying Scooter up under the dock. I had a sick feeling now why the Coast Guard hadn't wanted to get involved.

"Dick, you all right? You look like you've seen a ghost."

"Yeah, I just didn't think that...shit." I didn't want to tell her, but I didn't know what else I could say and not have her call me out on it right away, so I gave her the briefest of overviews surrounding Scooter's death.

Her reaction was exactly like that you'd expect from a pregnant woman whose husband just got called away on a secret mission and was now being told by someone she knew and trusted there was also a murder going on during it all that he might be a part of. "Do you think he might have had something to do with it?"

I told myself to sound sincere but not to oversell it. "Just the opposite. I think that might have been what they were called down there for, but by the time they got there the body had sunk, and it was chalked up to a misreport."

She grew terror stricken. "Maybe if he had gotten there faster he could have saved him."

I leaned over to do my best to reassure her that there was nothing he could have done, the whole time asking myself if it was something he could have been part of. "He would have known the priority from the phone call. If they had said 'rescue' he would have busted his hump to get there. They probably told him it was a 'recovery', something floating in the water."

"That's a harsh distinction."

"It's a harsh life." It was my turn to make overtures about it being time to leave, and she followed me to the door.

"Now what's next?

"For you I'm going to track down my friend, see what he knows about double secret missions in the Coast Guard. As for me, I guess I need to pay a visit to the boat in question."

"If you wait I can give you a ride back to the dock."

"No that's okay. It's a nice day for a walk, and a little exercise never hurt."

"Okay." Standing in the doorway, she seemed a little more concerned. "Promise me you'll let me know what you find out, in both cases."

"I will."

She lightened a little. "And please don't be so much of a stranger. I know," she touched my arm, "but you're the closest connection I have to him."

I had no words for that so I headed back to the waterfront. I'd like to tell you that I spent the walk wrapping my head around the fact that her husband might somehow be complicit in Scooter's death, but the reality was I was still thinking about the poem, specifically the second half she must have forgotten about:

> 'But if it had to perish twice,
> I think I know enough of hate
> To say that for destruction ice
> Is also great
> And would suffice.'

Old Frosty knew best: death comes no matter what climate you're living in.

Chapter 24

People tell stories about how their pets can sense that an earthquake is coming, know when their owner is sick or could even "see" ghosts. I don't know how much stock I put in the last one, but I firmly believe in the first two, with one small caveat:

It ain't just pets.

Animals are obviously still connected to nature. They know when to migrate, when to start storing nuts, how to find the stream they call home or the beach they were born on. It's only a small step to move from that to be able to feel faint rumbles in the earth or smell illness in the air. It's really no different than the gut feeling we get from time to time. Only thing is they get it all the time and are smart enough to pay attention to it.

Boats get left unattended down here for months at a time, and when the owners come back, there is barely a sign that a bird even flew overhead, much less took a break on deck looking for directions. Scooter hadn't even been dead a week and already his boat looked like a set piece from a remake of "The Birds." They knew he was gone for good so they were comfortable moving in. If they hadn't been there maybe I wouldn't have felt it, but with all those eyes bearing down on me I picked up on the sensation of death that clung to the boat.

A couple flew away as I came on deck but the rest of them knew that I was the stranger in a strange land, an intruder just passing through. They had arrived first so they claimed ownership. I tried to put them out of my mind and go about my job, knowing I already had two strikes against me.

Strike one was that I had no idea what I was looking for. I could count on exactly no fingers the number of times I had been on Scooter's boat, so unless it looked as if a rave had happened here I wouldn't know if anything was missing or out of place. My crime solving education came mostly from watching muted reruns of "Law & Order" on bar TV's, so unless Jerry Orbach or Sam Waterston magically showed up, I was pretty much at a loss.

Strike two came from the fact that whoever killed him certainly knew what he, she, it or they were doing, and I was guessing that included cleaning up after themselves. Realizing that gave me a chill. Were they watching the boat right now? They had left him to be found, but maybe his only purpose had been as bait, to see what else they could catch.

Suppose Scooter had secrets that they wanted and he felt like taking to his grave. Surely an investigation into his murder would turn up some of those secrets. This way they could get answers without having to put themselves any further into the mix. They would watch the investigation and try to connect the dots before the police do. If they had no problem getting rid of the person who had the secrets, I can't imagine they'd feel any qualms about taking out the patsy who unwittingly gave them the answers. Maybe just by standing on the boat I had marked myself as another loose end that would have to be tied up.

I didn't feel like making that third strike so I took a deep breath and started to focus. I had been in plenty of situations that had been far more stressful than this, and some of those had involved people who were about to die. Here, the guy was already dead. What could I possibly screw up?

I walked around the deck, trying to give everything a critical eye. It was hard to draw any conclusions because nothing seemed out of place. I took the lap as slowly as I could but was ready to give up and head below into the cabin when it dawned on me:

Nothing was out of place.

Most of the times I has seen Scooter out and about he was as close to being Pigpen from Charlie Brown as a nautical person could be. Slovenly, borderline unkempt, and perpetually confused where he left his drink or cigarettes, there is no way I could believe he kept his home life any neater, and certainly this precise was beyond explanation. Very few people are OCD enough to keep their house perfectly decorated; to achieve this state on a boat is impossible, but that was exactly what they had set out to do. They had taken the trouble to make it look like it had just been another day, nothing to see here, move along please.

No matter how hard you try to make something look casual and lived in, the only way it will look authentic is to actually live in it for a while. My guess was there had been a struggle, and after they had loaded Scooter onto their boat, they wanted to fix the mess. Problem was they hadn't paid enough attention to what it had looked like when they arrived so they erred on the side of caution. This way it may not look like how Scooter normally decorated – and they might also be betting on the fact that everyone was like me and had no idea for sure – but at least it didn't look like the scene of a fight. Now I just had to figure out where the fight started.

The cabin looked a lot more like I expected it to: unkempt and cluttered, with undertones of hoarding. Seeing the room the way I was supposed to was like night and day from my experience on the deck. In a glance I could tell everything was where it normally lived, or at least where he had casually dropped it. The only show of attention was a small area cleared on the table top. There were several small brushes and some silvery paint stains. My guess was maybe his hobby was model making, but there were no completed models to be seen. On my way out I noticed some fishing poles and a large tackle box, but the only things inside of them were more of the fishing weights. Hadn't this guy ever heard of a lure?

At least I knew that Scooter had been on deck when he, she, it or they had showed up, and he hadn't made it downstairs to hide and they hadn't gone down looking for anything. If they had, they knew they could have gotten away with leaving the deck a mess and it would fit right in. Of course, if they hadn't been looking for anything, it meant they hadn't showed up just to rob Scooter.

It meant they had come here to kill him.

Chapter 25

Whatever woke me up in the middle of the night was not
going to let me get back to sleep. That didn't surprise me
nearly as much as the fact that I had fallen asleep so soundly
in the first place. Whatever questions I had to face I had put
aside for a while, but now they were back and they were
setting down roots.

I stretched out on the pulpit of the boat counting what
stars I could see. Half a moon gives out a tenth the glow that
the full moon seems to, but most of the light pollution came
from the lamps dotting the streets and hotels that flank the
water's edge. Constellations came to me half finished, the
claws of Scorpio on stark relief against the darkened sky but
the stinger lost in an ugly haze. It was like a tide at the
horizon of the cosmos, and I wondered how long it would
take until people finally said enough, and I wondered where
I would be when that happened.

The stillness of the night was gently pushed away by the
sound of the world's slowest wake lapping against the side
of the boat. It was followed by the unmistakable bump of an
awkward body as he tried to orient himself. It did me no
good to look at him – I could never tell if he even had lips,
much less if they moved when he was talking – so I
concentrated on what stars I could see until he blew the
seawater out of his nose and started to speak.

"You didn't expect it to be a robbery, did you really?"

"I don't think it was a robbery, no."

"But..."

"But they didn't just go there to kill him, either. If that had been the case, you would have been the one to find him floating somewhere in the middle of nowhere long before he showed up where I could see him."

"Maybe they didn't have the right boat, or enough time."

"They certainly had the time, and they must have had the materials. Fastening him down the way they did certainly shows they had the time and skills."

I felt him scratch himself against the side of the boat while he thought about the evidence. "So narrow it down."

"A robbery gone sour or a generic killing is eliminated because the body is found. But if it's a premediated murder to send a message, he either needs to be someone important, which he's not, or have something they want so badly that the only way they can think to secure it is kill him."

"Still doesn't explain the way his body was found, and they didn't take anything off of the boat. At least not in a way to leave any clues behind."

"Maybe whatever they were interested in was up on the deck."

"Think of all the valuable things you own, and think of how many of them you keep on deck."

He was right. I didn't have all those hidden storage compartments just so my most valuable possessions would be out for people to see. Unless it was something he was trying to hide in plain sight.

"It wasn't that," he said, reading the thought. "He knew that what the people were looking for was something they would find no matter where it was."

"Still, it doesn't make sense."

"So go back to what's left. If they didn't kill him because of what he had, maybe they did it because of who he was."

He swam underwater, which was good because that way

he couldn't hear me snicker at the suggestion. I had only mentioned it at all so I could dismiss it. Scooter was a nobody, a curmudgeonly old crank who lived on a sailboat and pissed off his neighbors. In the three days he's been dead I've heard twice as many people confess to the killing. Yeah, people wanted him dead because of who he was, but they were all so proud of it they would have stood over the body for everyone to see.

He broke the surface and his voice filled my other ear. "It's important to you that it be an assassination."

"Why?"

"Because the other thought hits too close to home."

At first I thought he meant about robbery being part of the motive. There's a reason I've kept a low profile in the world. But it didn't make sense because whoever the killers were, they weren't interested in secrets, and I told him so.

"Maybe not secrets you can touch, but the kind of secrets you can share."

"Do you really think Scooter had any secrets to share?"

"Do you think anyone knows you have secrets?" Touché. "But that isn't what scares you. What scares you is this: he died alone, on a boat, and nobody missed him, saw him get taken or even cared that he was gone. Remind you of how anyone else might end up?"

I wanted to put that thought out of my mind right away, and I found a quick way to do it. "Yeah, but I don't expect to be trussed up under a dock after it happens."

"Interesting," he said as he started to swim away. "Makes you wonder if they knew exactly who it was going to be that found him."

Chapter 26

I was still staring at the sky when the sun came up several hours later. That fat bastard had a great way of leaving me with a thought so dark it made me long for the days of the bogeyman in the closet.

I was warned when I retired that too much time alone with myself could be a dangerous thing. That was exactly what I had wanted: time alone. I wanted to get as far away from the darkness of my past life and the demons that came with it. Last night in the starlight I realized that some of it had come with me, no matter how hard I tried to leave it behind. Maybe they were right. Maybe it was time I got a hobby, a different one from solving murders.

The sun chased away the darkness in my mind just as effectively as it washed away the night. Getting my fears out of the way let me get my focus back on Scooter. There had to be something that I wasn't seeing. It didn't matter that I didn't know what I was looking for; surely something was going to stick out. My past life may not have had anything to do with dead bodies – okay, not too much with them anyway – but powers of observation should be the same no matter what you're looking at.

Anyone who was thorough enough to stage the body the way they had could certainly be meticulous enough to clean up after themselves. But it was more than that. It was that they could take the time to do it. That had been one of the dark thoughts that kept coming back to me all night. It isn't just that living out here meant that most of your neighbors couldn't see what you were doing. It meant that those few who could see usually didn't care.

A person is sitting on their boat, minding their own business, when they see a dinghy pull up to Scooter's boat. Maybe they're curious, maybe they watch for a bit, but everyone out here is out here for a reason, and those reasons are usually best kept to themselves. There certainly is a sense of camaraderie among the live-aboards, some a little uneasier than others, but it comes with an understanding: you stay out of my shit and I'll stay out of yours. Who Scooter entertains is no business of theirs.

Anyway, it's a moot point: who abducts a person in broad daylight? Noises at night may raise questions, but sounds on the water have a habit of seemingly come from all over the place. Daylight brings vision into the equation, and it's hard to make a fight look like anything but.

Unless there wasn't a fight.

That thought sat me upright and looked to where Scooter's boat was. Maybe the reason nothing looked out of place was because nothing was. Scooter might have actually had friends. Well, "friends" is a strong word perhaps, seeing what they did to him, but maybe he at least knew who they were.

Maybe he had even been expecting them.

Chapter 27

The birds were still there when I showed up. But they seemed to know this time I wasn't coming aboard. The first time they squawked at me to let me know I was intruding; this time they barely even made a peep. They kept a wary eye on me as they warmed their wings in the sun but beyond that we paid each other scant attention. I pulled in as close as I could, but made no effort to reach for a tie line. Instead I started doing slow laps around the boat. I wasn't nearly as interested in what I could see as I was in who could see me.

Candy had said she'd seen Scooter at the end of her shift. While this gave me a general time frame of 3pm, I never asked if he was coming or going at the time. My gut told me he had just been getting to the bar at the time. Scooter had the type of personality that made people want to share with others how annoying he was; if he had been there for any part of her shift she probably would have told me.

Assuming he hadn't stayed long – an assumption based on nothing but hope – that only gave about a two hour window of daylight. Further compounding the issue is that I was out here at the wrong time of the day. Very few people who considered themselves morning people made it through the entire day without taking a nap. My most likely witnesses were probably still sleeping. Still, I was here now and determined to make the best out of it.

One of the charms people say Key West has is that you could be sitting at a bar with two people who are both dressed in what could be best described as "distressed casual." One of them could be flat broke and homeless while the other is a multimillionaire and you wouldn't be able to tell the difference. If you aren't looking carefully, the mooring field could appear the same way. There are certainly a couple of boats that look much nicer than others and a few that seem to be defying logic by still being afloat, but at a casual glance the rest wouldn't stick out of a line-up.

On my second pass I started to notice some of the differences. Call me prejudiced (go ahead, I'll wait) but it was the nicer looking ones that went to the top of my list. People who let their boats go might be in danger of also letting their minds go, and that was the reason I didn't want to do a neighborhood canvas in the first place. Nothing is more of a timewaster than listening to someone who earnestly believes that Bigfoot swam up on the back of the Loch Ness Monster and took Scooter away. For the rest of you, you'd be scared that kind of craziness might be contagious. As for me, let's just say that factually I know three reasons why that couldn't have happened.

I kept doing laps, making mental notes of where I might start. There were signs of life on a few boats, but the one that began to interest me the most was an older model cabin cruiser. The life there was pretty hard to see. From the corner of my eye the only movement I picked up on was the coffee cup going back and forth to her mouth. She was good enough to not even move her head as she tracked my progress. When I was confident it was more than just me being spooked by shadows I waited until I was on the far side of Scooter's boat and then hop-scotched a roundabout way, hoping to stay out of her line of sight.

I slid out of the lee side of a sailboat but all I saw was the empty chair where she had been sitting. It was possible that in my stealthy activities she had gotten bored of me and decided to move inside or head to shore. I figured that since I was here and she was still the best ticket I had in a long shot raffle I throttled up and headed to her stern. I was just tying off when I heard the familiar sound of a shot gun shell being loaded.

I looked into the double barrel of an old over/under Remington. She didn't hold the weapon like it was her first day picking it up, and she didn't seem overly nervous about who she was pointing it at. She was a woman who would shoot me once and not think about it twice. As slowly as I could, I stood to my full height, hands tentatively signaling she had indeed scored a touchdown.

"You ain't one of them, are you?"

"Well, I think not, thought I don't know who 'them' they are."

"No I suppose you're not." The gun dropped a little. "They were dressed way fancier than you."

"I don't even own a suit."

The gun moved backed up. "If you ain't them, how do you know they were wearing suits?"

I shuddered to think that this wasn't the first time my fool mouth was going to get me shot. "A lucky guess." I gestured at the gun, hoping for some levity. "A shot in the dark, you might say."

The gun didn't move. "No shot, no thump, no nothing. But all the same, I don't think he went willingly. Which leads me to guess that's why you're here."

"Yes ma'am. Just trying to find out what happened."

"You a cop?"

This was when I realized I should have taken the Chief up on his offer to deputize me. A half-assed badge is better than no badge at all. I thought about trying to bluff my way through this, but she had the look of someone who's called a lot of bluffs and never been wrong.

"No ma'am, I'm not."

"Good." The gun dropped completely. "Never been a fan of cops. Come on board and I'll tell you what I know." She stepped back to let me up the ladder. "And I appreciate the manners, but my mom made me call her 'ma'am' for the first seventeen years of my life. The day I turned eighteen I told her exactly where she could stuff that word. Name's Harper."

Chapter 28

I can't say that I would want to be on Harper's boat if we were trying to outrun a hurricane, or even a sea turtle, but what it lacked in apparent horsepower it made up for in certain charm and cleanliness. It had the well-worn look of a place that had been home for several years. As she made a fresh pot of coffee she told me enough of her story for me to gather she had been lucky enough to not have such a hard life after leaving home. The results of that life had been the opportunity to enjoy a comfortable Spartan retirement in Key West. But that wasn't the story I wanted to hear, and after she had poured the coffee and sat down I could tell it wasn't the story she wanted to tell.

"Friday afternoon he was just like clockwork. He'd try to tell you otherwise, mostly because that sour goat always had to be contrary, but he had a routine that was set in stone. I watched him go in the same time he always does, and figured I wouldn't see him again until the next morning."

"He usually stay out all night?"

"Nope, but late enough so the sun would be down."

"But you would know it was him."

"Sure. His dinghy had a bad spark plug. I could hear that engine cough a mile away. That was why I thought it was strange when I heard it maybe only an hour or so later.

"I was sitting on the sunset side reading when I heard it. Think what you want, but I'm a curious person. I've been watching him long enough to know he never changes his patterns. So I slipped across the deck, acted like I was fixing dinner, and kept a casual eye on him.

"He barely had enough time to go below deck and get changed before this other dinghy pulls up. I recognize Smitty from the fuel dock, but the other two looked like a cross between Jehovah's Witnesses and the IRS. They hop off and Smitty doesn't wait around."

"Can't imagine you heard what they said to each other."

"Didn't have to. It was one of the strangest scenes I've ever witnessed. They all looked relaxed, but none of them looked friendly."

"I don't follow."

"There were no handshakes or anything. I definitely got the impression that Scooter didn't want them there, but he seemed awfully casual about them being on his boat."

"Maybe he didn't think he could do anything about it."

She shook her head. "I wish I didn't know this, but I do: when Scooter wants something he has a way of making it happen. If he really wanted them gone, I don't think they would have gotten there in the first place.

"The visitors make themselves a drink, Scooter fixes himself one, and the three of them proceed to do almost nothing. I can see them gesturing to each other from time to time, but they never raise their voices or nothing. I tell you, if it hadn't been such an abrupt change in his schedule I would have paid it no mind at all. The birds on his boat now are more entertaining than those three were. Eventually even the novelty of Scooter having friends wore off, and after about an hour I went back to my book."

"Until after sunset when you heard his dinghy."

"Once the sun goes down Smitty ain't taking anybody anywhere, so I wasn't surprised, seeing as how he was their only way back to town. Didn't even think much about when I hadn't heard him come back before I fell asleep. I just figured that maybe they found a way to have more fun on the island than they did on the boat."

Harper was certainly far sharper than anyone I hoped to find, so I decided to press my luck. "Based on what you saw, what kind of relationship do you think the three of them had?"

She thought about it for a minute. "I almost think it was like they didn't have a relationship. More like people who only have one thing in common, like co-workers who run into each other outside of the workplace." She thought more and a smile came to her face. "Not just any place, but like a doctor's office, where they can't leave because they are all waiting for an appointment."

Seemed like my hunches were paying off. If she was right, then he did know them and knew that this meeting was an eventuality, even if he wasn't too keen on hanging out with them. One of my next steps was to meet this Smitty guy, but I had a new question before I left.

"If you don't mind me saying this Harper, you seem like you got a lot more to offer this world then just watching the comings and goings of your neighbor."

"You probably do too, and yet here we are talking about him."

"I guess life gives us odd situations that change us."

For the first time since I met her, her face fell just a little and she cast her eyes down. "Remember when I said Scooter could always get what he wanted?"

"Yeah."

"Years ago, it seems he wanted me. And he got it. Even if I didn't want to give it to him."

"I'm sorry."

"Yeah, well," and her face came up, set now in anger. "That's more than he ever said. But me, I was the most sorry,

sorry that I let it happen."

"Hey, c'mon, you know it isn't your fault." I may have been underqualified to investigate a murder, but I felt like Perry Mason in comparison to my qualifications as a rape counsellor. I wasn't sure how to best comfort or reassure her, but I realized it didn't matter. Time had galvanized this episode a particular way in her memory, and nothing was going to change it. "I'm not saying I haven't made mistakes in my life, but it had been a long time. Maybe I let my guard down, gone soft, but I was so mad at myself I didn't know what to do. So I waited and I watched.

"After I realized he understood that to try it again would be foolish, I came up with a new plan. Every day I thought about it, about how it would go down and how it would make me feel."

My skin crawled a little in a sudden chill. "I don't suppose that plan had anything to do with two guys in dark suits."

"Nothing that complicated."

"Well, would you mind filling in an amateur sleuth?"

She got up from her chair and disappeared. When she came back the shot gun had been replaced with a pistol. Without hesitating she drew a bead on a bird perched on Scooter's chair. She pulled the trigger and the bird exploded.

Suddenly the air was filled with the screams of hundreds of frightened birds. I looked around but either nobody heard the gun shot or cared that much about it. The fear passed quickly through the brain pans of the birds and they settled back to their new home. I turned to Harper who was silently crying.

"Every day I thought about doing it, but I just couldn't bring myself to. I kept thinking that we were both to blame, and if I killed him wouldn't I be killing a part of me to, a part he had already attacked? And now that he's dead, I don't know if I should be happy somebody killed him or angry that I couldn't bring myself to do it myself."

Chapter 29

Despite the one enormous emotional elephant in her room, Harper seemed like someone who would be good to know. As I motored towards the fueling dock I decided I would swing by every so often. I also decided I would announce my approach and intentions before I got too close.

I felt a little inadequate pulling up between two sixty foot yachts in my six foot dinghy, but I comforted myself by remembering that I had nothing I needed to compensate for. There was a kid scampering around the pumps and I told him I was looking for Smitty.

"That's me."

"Can't be. Smitty's an old man's name. What are you, seventeen?"

"I'm twenty two."

"Don't lie to me kid. I'm not the bartender you have to convince."

"Whaddya want?"

"Tell me about the two guys you gave a lift to last Friday afternoon."

His face lit up. "Oh man, I've been keeping an eye out for them. They need something?"

'Yeah, an alibi and an explanation,' I thought, but all I said out loud was "Don't know. I'm trying to track them down myself. Why you so interested in seeing them again?"

He sat down on the edge of the dock so he could whisper. "Here's how it goes. People come up here and the first three words out of their mouth are always 'How much for?'

Doesn't matter what it's for. Not only do they know everything has a price, they also know how the game is played."

"Game?"

"Sure. They say 'How much for a ride to Christmas Tree Island?' I say 'We don't do that.' They say 'Twenty bucks.' I tell them I could get in trouble, so they up it to thirty. I mention that my boss would need a cut, and the next thing you know I got two twenty dollar bills in my pocket for a ten minute job."

"Minus your boss's cut."

Smitty laughed. "Are you kidding? He doesn't know. I have a sign that says 'Back in five' and nobody says nothing."

"Uh-huh. And I'm guessing these two guys didn't know the game."

"They walk up to me and don't ask anything. They say 'Take us out to a boat' and hand me this." He pulled a crisp hundred dollar bill from his pocket. "I'm afraid to spend it just in case it might be fake."

I held out my hand and after a second he figured he could trust me to examine it. "Did they tell you they were going to see Scooter?"

"They never said his name but as soon as they described the boat I knew it was his. He really dead?"

"As dead as he can be. Just like this is as real as it can be." I handed it back to him and pushed off from the dock. "Go get drunk tonight kid."

"Thanks. If I see you tonight, maybe I'll buy you a drink."

And most likely I would say yes, because I had a feeling I was going to need one. I throttled up with the intention of heading back to the hospital. One thing I hadn't thought to look for was if there had been any defensive wounds.

Just because you work with people doesn't mean you'd go somewhere with them without first putting up a fight.

As I swung around I saw that my plans might have to wait another day. I knew a little rain wasn't going to hurt me, but that didn't mean I had to subject myself to it. Besides, Scooter's body wasn't going anywhere. Or so I thought.

Chapter 30

Seeing as how the Chief and I were now on somewhat civil terms I took the assumption that there would be no more unfriendly visits from the Coast Guard. That meant it seemed like as good a time as any to replenish what they had taken away. Had they been serious during their visit, or had my skin been darker or my name sounded like one you'd associate with a taco truck, they would have sent someone down to where I was now: knee deep in grease and grime crawling around my engine compartment.

Mine was probably a bit cleaner than most, seeing as how I couldn't remember the last time I had run the engine. Still, it was a hot dirty place and I wasn't a fan of being down there. I was trying to decide just how much I should take with me so I wouldn't have to visit again too soon when a somewhat familiar voice made the decision for me.

"Excuse me, Mr. Lockhart? Anyone home?"

"Yup. Just give me a minute." I pulled myself up, replaced the hatch and tried to wipe off some of the dusty dirt from my hands, just in case this was a formal visit involving handshakes. I slid the package into a tucked away compartment and came up on deck.

"Twice in twenty minutes Smitty. I'm starting to think you might have a crush on me."

"You came to me first, mister." He had his hand on the tiller and a slightly nervous looking Dr. White in the bow of the boat."

"Not much of a seagoing guy, are you?"

"Morgues don't float, and I've no interest in working a cruise ship."

"You coming aboard?"

"No." He answered quickly, more as if the thought of having to get off the dinghy scared him than of anything else. "I'm actually on my way back up to the mainland. Just wanted to come by and tell you that."

"Dr. Santacrose is back?"

"He will be tomorrow and I guess they figured since one bizarre murder already happened this week, there won't be another for at least eighteen hours."

"I'm glad you told me all this, saves me a trip."

"Why is that?"

"With everything else that had been done to him, did you see any signs of a struggle?"

"You mean, besides a tube being forcibly shoved down his throat?"

When he put it that way, it made my question sound kind of dumb, but it had been asked. "Well, yeah."

Turns out it was only a dumb question because he hadn't even thought to look. Now I understood why he was having a hard time finding a full-time job. "It didn't seem like something to think about. To me it looked straightforward: he got drugged and he got weighted." He looked at Smitty and then back at me. "I guess we can go back and take a look, but I was kind of hoping to beat the traffic."

Dedicated professional, that's what I liked about him. "No, it's fine. I can take a look tomorrow." The clouds that had loomed before now threatened and I was in the mood to get stuck in only one type of place when the rains came. I waved him off. "Drive safe."

I didn't wait for a reply because I didn't think there'd be one coming that I needed to hear, but I was wrong. "Thanks.

I may have missed the wounds but I didn't miss the water."

"What?"

"The water in his lungs was fresh water, and the water only would have gotten there if he had still been alive when he'd gone under."

"That's not possible. Unless we're wrong about the amount of time he spent marinating."

"I checked on that again as soon as I saw the water. The body definitely spent between sixty six and seventy two hours in the water."

"Are you telling me that they kidnapped him, tortured him, put him in a bathtub or pool until they were sure he was dead, and then dumped him in the harbor?"

Smitty managed to look pale beneath his tan and Dr. White nodded his head. "That's about the long and short of it. And before you ask, there isn't much of a way to tell how long he was in one and how long he was in the other. Once you're dead, you stop taking on water."

"Best you could hope for," I ventured, "was to estimate based on how bitten up he looked from the harbor wildlife."

"Oh sure. Of course, that means you'd have to know how much wildlife we're talking about, how hungry they are, how often they feed and any number of other factors. I don't suppose you have that information handy."

I didn't, but I know someone who might. Problem is he avoided being in the harbor during the rain just as much as I did. The doc continued to talk.

"On the bright side, if there is one, is that at least it doesn't change too much about the case for you."

"No, I guess it doesn't. Thanks for your help doc."

"Good luck." With that Smitty knew the visit was over and he turned them back to land. I went back below deck to change clothes and think about how wrong the doc was.

Knowing that he wasn't dumped right away meant that he could have been dumped at any time. Scooter's friends had sat on the body long enough to know when the best time to ditch the body would be. Question was what constituted the best time?

When they knew nobody would see them, or when they could guarantee who would find the body?

Chapter 31

It's easy to pick out the newbies from the veterans. Newbies don't own pants. When people first get to the island they can't imagine how anybody could find 65 degrees cold, and when they're only here for a week they never find out. Exception is when the weather is exceptional, and not in a good way. Then it seems like they go out of their way to make sure everyone knows how cold it is.

I threw on jeans and grabbed a long sleeved shirt before I headed into town. I know I wasn't doing myself any favors by going to an outdoor bar, but at least the Pelican Deck is blocked off from the wind and has plenty of covered seating. Besides I know that, short of a hurricane, the musicians would still be there, and nothing sucks worse than playing to an empty house.

The sky hadn't been too long in making good with its promise and by the time I got to the alley fat drops were beginning to explode off the pavement. I picked up my pace just in case they all decided to fall at once. As expected there weren't more than a handful of people there, and except for three girls looking to make the best of a bad situation, I knew every one of them. I had to. Most of them had already confessed to me. On the bright side, Clint Bullard was the musician, and even on a slow wet afternoon between the songs he song and the stories he told, he seemed to make miserable days seem much less so.

There's a science to everything and that includes the stool you take at the bar. I took a seat on the front corner so I could watch the stage and turn my head for Yeddie's attention but not have to be drawn into any conversations I didn't want to be part of. It seemed like everyone was in the same no talkative mood I was in. Yeddie greeted me with a beer, a shot and a nod, before drifting off to the other end of the bar. It wasn't that far too drift, and there was nothing needing his attention, but it didn't matter to me. Before he made it that far I was already off in my own world.

With a rain heavy cloud cover it gets hard to tell when the hours have passed: various shades of grey don't have the same contrast as light blue going to crimson red before becoming saturated purple. Clint was still singing so it couldn't have gotten that late, but I realized I hadn't really looked at anything other than him or the inside of my own thoughts when I saw an unmistakable gait from the corner of my eye.

One the scale of people in my life, with Scooter at the bottom and Yeddie and Mike near the top, Frankie Go Funny exists somewhere in the middle. He has an unenviable ability to make you want to kill him and then restoring your faith in him, and humanity, before the night is over. As you can imagine, such a personality could be hard to deal with when not in the mood. It isn't that I hated him, or even disliked him, but he could damn sure make me wish I took a left instead of a right once upon a time in my life.

He drew my full attention and that gave me a reason to look around the bar again. The rain had tapered off but the air was still heavy with moisture. People had finally decided this was about as good as it was going to get today and had filled up the bar nicely. I saw some more faces I knew, many I didn't, and a few that fell in between. What I didn't see much of were empty stools, with the exception of one near me, so I turned my attention towards the bar and hoped he would miss me. Par for the course my life had been playing on lately, he didn't.

At the same time he placed a hand on my back he said "Hey Tricky Tick, how is the world treating you? I trust that life has been well, in spite of the recent demise of Scooter and your subsequent position as chief investigator into such matters. No worries, because I, like all of my island brethren, are full of the utmost faith that you will bring this drama to a swift and conclusive conclusion. Now, may I sponsor you to a dram or two of your favorite libation whiles you and I converse?"

Well, that was what he possibly would have said, although not likely. Knowing how his mind worked, odds are he would have said something much closer to "Hey Tricky Tick, how's tricks?" The thing is, he never got a chance to say anything after the words "Hey Tricky Tick." It's a Pavlovian response. If anyone other than my ex-wife calls me by the nickname that she gave me, I punch them in the throat.

If you can look beyond the violence it's actually kind of impressive. I hear the words, I swing without aiming, and yet I never come in too high or too low. I guess I'm lucky enough to not come in too hard either, because I know I could end up doing serious damage. That's not my intention at all. I'm just looking to shut them up, because I figure if they're dumb enough to say that, whatever else comes out of their mouth will only be dumber.

He had already started to settle his weight onto his stool when I made contact, so I could feel him try to gain some balance as his body shifted beneath him. A few people looked over, their attention dragged more by his seal-like coughing than his physical manifestations. If Clint had been between songs more people might have been interested, but

I guess I was going to be at least a little lucky in all of this. By the time he managed to regain himself and sit down, Yeddie had come over.

"Why on Earth would you call him that?"

"Cause I thought it would be funny."

"Betcha you're gonna stop thinking that."

Frankie turned to me. "I'm guessing this ain't the first time someone called you that."

"No, but it's the first time someone's called me that in over a dozen years." At least to my face. My ex-wife might call me that every day, if she's even still thinking about me, but mutual thousand yard restraining orders make family reunions hard to organize.

"Maybe it's time we bring it back!" He was sincerely excited about the concept, which should be enough to demonstrate my description of him. I shifted back in my seat, as much to watch the musician as to make sure he knew I wasn't fucking around.

"Now that Scooter's dead, I'm looking for someone to like the least on this island. Call me that again and you'll go immediately to the head of the class." I finished pivoting away from the bar and saw myself looking at one of the semi-familiar faces I had seen earlier.

My friends from Miami were back, and they looked none too happy to see me.

Chapter 32

"Making fun of tourists and beating up cripples. I guess those are your hobbies." (Hey, look at that. I do have hobbies after all!) "Pretty lousy hobbies if you ask me."

"How many bars did you have to visit before the bartenders finally explained what MDT meant and didn't just laugh at you?"

"Only one, because they were smart enough not to fuck with me."

"Guess that makes me not very bright."

"Or tough, swinging at cripples like this.

Frankie got off his stool and stood next to me. "Call me cripple again and you'll be walking a lot funnier than me."

(Now's probably as good a time as any to explain Frankie's nickname. At some point as a child, he did something to his leg, and now his left foot is kind of like a lazy eye. It doesn't focus where the rest of him does, but it also doesn't stop him from getting where he's going. How it happened is pretty unimportant, for no other reason than Frankie makes it so. Over the years I've heard him blame a dog, a lawn mower, a bicycle and a busted storm drain. With so many different culprits I'm guessing the real reason is something he doesn't want to think about.)

"You're actually friends with this broken down dead beat?" I'm guessing my Miamian friend didn't know that people could have a complex relationship. Frankie wasn't taking the bait, but he also wasn't getting me off the hook entirely.

"It's a small island, so our choices are limited. But I'd rather hang out with a dozen of him than one of you."

Since Frankie wouldn't be his ally, he decided to turn on him. "You must be more of a cripple than I thought if you think this guy is worth your time."

Frankie moved even closer and could have licked the guy's mustache if he wanted to. Of course to do so he'd have to bend over a few inches. People have a bad habit of seeing Frankie's leg and assuming anyone with an injury like that couldn't possibly be 6'4" and pushing 275. "I'm pretty sure I told you not to use that word again."

Clint was between songs and he realized there was better entertainment going on at the bar than anything he could provide on stage. His watching us made other people turn their attention, and even though more tourists had filtered in over the last couple of hours, there was still a healthy amount of locals, which was a good thing. Out-of-towners have no dog in a fight like this, but locals know exactly whose side they are on. You could get a hundred people who can't stand each other, but give them one common enemy from somewhere else and suddenly you're filming a remake of "Band of Brothers."

Even the biggest guy will pay attention to the numbers game, and the Miamian realized he had bitten off far more than he could chew right now. Still, he wasn't going to go out with his tail between his leg and he turned to face me.

"I got four more days on my vacation, and if you're smart enough to have this" I could tell he wanted to say cripple, but that he also wanted to keep his balls "guy as your friend, then you'd be smart enough to not let him out of your sight those next four days. Cause the minute you do, I'm gonna be there, and I'm coming after you."

My eyes stared straight ahead, but my words weren't for

him. "You hear that, Go Funny? Sounds like you just got nominated to be my personal ass wiper."

"Just as long as you don't expect me to shake you junk when you're done taking a leak."

That broke the crowd up, and Clint, god bless his entertainer's timing, picked up on the laughter to further defuse the situation. He hit the opening chord and first lines of "The Road Goes On Forever" and the crowd instantly turned back to him and started to sing along. A half dozen or so locals stayed where they were while the Miamian and his posse made for the exit. There were a couple nods of acknowledgement as we all moved back to wherever we had been. Frankie slid on the stool next to me, this time smart enough not to try a nickname.

A couple of stools down some crusty kid was watching over our shoulders as they left. "People like that piss me off. They ruin everything."

Normally I don't engage people in such conversations, especially people who are far too young to have experienced enough to have formed an uninformed opinion, but my feathers were already ruffled so I was feeling frisky. "Yeah? How do they do that?"

"These jokers are the people responsible for killing Key West. They come down here and don't give a crap about the local community. They want to make sure they have all the creature comforts and brand names from home, and they don't care how much it costs to get it. It drives the prices up for everyone else and pretty soon nobody who makes this place authentic can afford to live here."

"Authentic, huh? How long has your family lived here?"

"My family?"

"Yeah, your family. I'm guessing you were born and raised here, since you know about what makes this island

126

authentic."

"Look man, just because I moved here three years ago doesn't mean I don't know what authentic is."

"You don't and neither does my friend Dick here," Frankie chimed in. "To be an authentic Key Westerner, you'd have to be a native of the Calusa tribe. Which would be pretty impressive, since those that weren't all but wiped out some 200 years ago were moved to Cuba, and I bet you couldn't find Cuba on a map even if you were given a missile crisis and a cigar head start."

This was when I realized I really like Go Funny, because not only was he great at putting douche nozzles in their place, he did it with just enough of a smile on his face that most of them wouldn't realize he was dressing them down until the next day.

"But you know what I'm saying. Look at how expensive rents have become. Look how chain brands are driving out local institutions. Do we really need five drug stores on a ten block stretch of Duval Street?"

"Maybe not," Go Funny admitted, "but do you know what we do need?"

"What?"

"People like him." He hiked a thumb towards the door.

"How the fuck can you say that?"

I knew where Frankie was going and I took over. "What's your name?"

"Jonah."

I skipped the whale reference and moved on. "What do you do for a job Jonah?"

"I work doing Jet Ski tours."

Go Funny and I shared an eye-roll. In the pantheon of things brought to the island that people cited as ruining the quality of life, Jet Skis usually showed up near the top of the list.

"How many people you think you get a week on your tour?"

"You can't really say that. I mean, it varies from week to week and even day to day, you know?" Which was a polite way of saying he didn't have a clue in the world.

"Humor me. Pick a number. I'm not going to run out to the harbor next week and count, just to see if you're right."

"Couple hundred I guess."

"And of all those couple hundred, how many of them are locals, and how many are out-of-towners?"

One of the things I love is when you can absolutely hear someone smiling next to you, and that's exactly what Go Funny was doing right before he spoke. "And I'm guessing those day to day fluctuations are caused primarily by cruise ships in town. Big boat comes in means big trips for Jonah."

"And no boats means no trips," I finished off. "So, locals versus tourists, what's your guess?"

Jonah finally picked up where we were going and said nothing, but Go Funny wasn't going to let him off the hook. "If it weren't for people like that, people you can't stand, people who are ruining this place, you'd have no job. Which I guess makes you part of the problem."

Jonah suddenly had friends anywhere else on the island and threw some money on the bar before walking away. "Kid's a politician in the making," Frankie said.

"How you figure that? Politicians are supposed to be likeable."

"He could be likeable enough to the right people. Politicians these days, they don't understand what compromise is. They want things to be exactly the way they want it and nothing else. He's the same way. He wants his world to be only his way. Doesn't understand you got to give a little, bend a little, so you can have what you want."

"Balance."

"Exactly. I'd like a lot of the people who come here on vacation to go somewhere else, but I also like not having to subsist on palm fronds and rain water, you know? That's why retired bastards like you have it so easy."

"I don't know if easy is what I'd call it all the time."

"Hell, you at least got it easier than Scooter." He picked up his drink and pivoted on his stool. For a minute I was afraid I was Father Flannigan and it was confession time again, but he just kept turning, leaning his elbows on the bar and listening about Sherry and Sonny. "Then again, maybe not. I guess it doesn't get much easier than being dead."

Chapter 33

Selective hearing goes a long way towards enjoying life in Key West. I have nothing against the outside talkers who work Duval Street. We all have a job to do. Well, most of us anyway. But there's a lot of them and so I tune them out. Especially the strip bar that sits diagonally from the Pelican on the corner of Duval. Of course, they're probably about as interested in me as I am in them. I know what they have to offer and I know when to find it when I'm in the mood.

It wasn't the droning baritone voice of hot naked women and cold AC that broke through my defenses but the lilt of a false soprano. "Hey sailor, can I buy you a drink?" She didn't wait for an answer but just hooked my arm in hers and we crossed over to Alan's Crab Shack. Silly name for a bar that hadn't served crabs in years, but what are you gonna do? We pushed our way through the karaoke kids up front to the quieter back bar. Another good thing about living here: tourists buy drinks for strippers, but strippers buy drinks for locals.

As far as I knew her name was Scarlett. Could be true, could be one she made up for her job. I figured if it wasn't who she was she would tell me if she wanted to. I had a feeling I knew more about her than most people did, mostly because she told me this, but there was still a lot I didn't know, and we both seemed comfortable about that. If this is the part where I'm supposed to tell you about her being the stripper with the heart of gold, well, I don't know much about that, but I do know the two moneymakers that covered her heart didn't come cheap.

"Slow night?"

"Slow enough. Too many girls trying to work too hard, so I'm fine taking a break now and then."

"Yeah but you don't get paid drinking with me."

"I also don't get paid grinding for mid-week coupon clippers either. I'm all about the quality, not the quantity."

I couldn't argue about an efficient worker. She took a long pull from her drink before lighting a cigarette. "I'm glad I ran into you. Have I got a story for you!"

'Shit,' I thought. 'Here we go again.' "Let me guess, this is about Scooter?"

"Who?" The blank stare let me know she wasn't pulling my leg.

"Scooter. The old guy who drowned over the weekend. Lived on a boat, pissed everyone off, found him under the dinghy dock at Barnacle Bob's, that guy?"

She shrugged her shoulders in a way that painfully reminded me how young she was. Not many years ago that was the same shrug her father got when he asked if she'd had friends over while he'd been out of town.

"Be glad you didn't. I'm sure glad you are because everybody else has wanted to talk to me about him."

"I promise you this has nothing to do with him."

"Fire away then."

"Saturday night, I get done about midnight, head home, get changed and head out to the C Note. Find a spot in the corner, away from the pool table and most of the jokers and just unwind with a drink. Well, not long after I get there, this guy walks in, and he's about as out of place as a white sheet salesman at an NAACP rally. The only thing that didn't make him totally uncomfortable was that he had loosened his tie just a little."

"Maybe he was the last man standing from a wedding party."

She shook her head. "Wrong kind of suit. This was a business suit all the way, but one that looked like it came off the discount rack. He didn't really look around much but just sat at the first stool he could find and ordered a drink.

"I couldn't tell what he was drinking but he must have liked them because he was on his third in about ten minutes. Between his hollow leg and his horrible fashion sense he was easily the most interesting person in the room, and I couldn't help myself. I moved over to where he was and took the empty stool next to him at the bar.

"He looked me over real quick, just like you would anyone else sit that close to you, nothing more, and went back to his drink. I really don't know what came over me. I mean, I'm not a fan of talking to guys when I'm getting paid to do it, why should I care about doing it for free? But something about the whole environment made it worth pursuing.

"'You look like you had a rough night.' I said. 'The only rough thing about it,' he replied, 'was how boring it was. And I have to do it all over again tomorrow.'

"I said something about us all not being able to have glamorous jobs and asked him what kind of work he did. When he told me asset recovery, I said the first thing that popped into my mind: 'Down here we call them treasure hunters.'

"Dick, I wish I could explain the look in his eye. Thing was I barely saw it at first. I kept rambling on about how treasure hunting was pretty much about as exciting as it got, and if his job wasn't exciting maybe he needed to start looking for a different treasure, I don't know, I was just rambling, but then I looked and I saw it. I'm telling you if he had been just a bit more of an asshole or less intelligent he might have throttled me right there in the bar. Maybe he thought he was being funny when he said asset recovery, and maybe I guessed a little too close to home, but suddenly we both knew he was not a happy camper. I started talking even faster, saying something about the suit probably meant he was in management, that's why he was bored, that it was still nicer to have to get dressed up for work than to undress for work, did I tell you I was a stripper, hey you look ready for another drink, how about this weather were having. It's like my jaw just unhinged and words started spewing out.

"I guess he never actually met a stripper before because he started asking me about that, and even though I hate it, I felt the more he talked the less likely he'd be to kill, so I just started making up stories, saying whatever I could. He was starting to unwind, and I was hoping to maybe find a way to get myself out of this situation, so I suggested we head down to the pool table.

"Everybody there made fun of his suit but none of them asked what he did for a living, and that kept things on a lighthearted keel. I even saw him disappear out back with a couple of the guys and when he came back in I could tell he wouldn't be getting much sleep before he had to work again the next day. I had to do the same, so that seemed like as good a time as any to leave.

"For some reason I felt like I had to say goodbye to him, even if I'd never see him again, and he thanked me for helping him relax and forget about work for a while. And then he slid something in my hand, said it was a gift and told me not to lose it. I felt the slickness of a glycine bag and, believe what you want, me and party favors don't mix. But I remembered that look in his eye and figured it'd be best to say thank you and ditch it on the walk home, which is what

I planned to do.

"Thing was as soon as I started walking home, I figured that no matter what it was, it was probably worth something, so why should I just throw the money away? I slid it into my pocket and actually almost forgot about it until I started getting undressed for bed."

She reached into her purse and slid the bag on the bar for me to look at. "Is that really what I think it is?"

I picked up the bag to get a better look. There was almost no weight to it and when I held it up to the light I could actually see the light through it. I placed the bag between two of my finger tips and very gently started to curl the bag. The gold flake curled along with it.

"Sure looks like it is."

"How much do you think it's worth?"

"Couple hundred bucks maybe. You'd need to weigh it out for sure. You got any friends in the jewelry business down here?"

"Only most of them," she answered with a smile, showing off a stunning diamond tennis bracelet. "Remember, I work for quality." She threw some money on the bar. "Need to get back to work. Thanks for the company."

"Thanks for the drinks. I'll walk you out. I need to get up pretty early tomorrow anyway."

"What's early for you? Eleven a.m.?"

It used to be, but lately that hadn't even been a day of sleeping in. Plus she might know something else that would make me have to get up even earlier than I was already planning.

"Ten forty-five. Let me ask you something," I said when we got back onto the street. "Your man in the ill-fitting suit. Did you see him again?"

"Nope. Told me he would try to come in on Sunday evening, but never showed."

"I don't suppose he told you where he was staying."

"The Shipyard. Why you so interested? He a friend of yours?"

"More like a friend of a friend."

"That Scooter guy?"

"Exactly." I gave her a kiss on the cheek. "Go have fun fleecing the sheep," and she disappeared into the crowd. Looks like not only was I going to have to get up early, but for the second day in a row I was going to be going door to door.

I'm telling you, my luck just keeps getting better and better.

Chapter 34

It might have been a shipyard once upon a time, but that would have been a couple hundred years and a half mile of landfill ago. Now it was just another condo development that wouldn't have looked out of place almost anywhere else in the country, the only difference being pricy property meant no wasted space.

Another thing there wasn't was a centralized rental office I could go asking questions in. Many of the condos were second homes, used mostly to rent to other people for their vacations, and handled through a variety of websites and management companies. Wouldn't much matter if I had a place to go anyway. What was I supposed to say? "Hi, I'm looking for a couple of guys who may or may not have been wearing off the rack suits from Sears, but with a bad attitude. They were here, somewhere, last weekend, and before you ask, no I have no actual authority to be doing this search."

The one thing left in my favor was that in a complex full of transients most people wouldn't mind talking to a stranger about the strangers that had been near them. I wandered back onto one of the secluded sidewalks to see what I could scare up.

If the coroner was right, and they had been sitting on the body here in a bathtub, then I had at least a better than average chance they'd been seen at different times of the day. I can't imagine hired killers would have made a stop at the grocery store in order to stock up for the week, which meant trips in and out of the complex looking for a neighborhood store. The place was still quiet but on a corner unit that looked bigger than most I found a guy drinking coffee and scrolling through his phone.

"Excuse me, buddy, you got a light?" Once upon a time this was the perfect ice breaker because if the person you were talking to didn't smoke, the person next to them did. Now I was just as likely to get a lecture about all the perils of smoking and what a horrible creature I was, polluting the world, as I was a dumb stare, but I was sure this guy could help me out. The bong I saw through the window was not self-lighting.

Without looking up he dug the lighter out of his pocket and tossed it in the direction of my voice. When I was done, he still was not interested in looking at me, which made returning the lighter difficult. I guess his coffee was strong enough to make him a mind reader.

"Just toss it on the table top."

"Thanks, but I was hoping I could ask you another favor."

"Nope."

Another one of our post-modern charm school graduates. Great. "I just need a couple of questions answered. You'd be helping me out a lot."

His response this time was even brusquer. I hadn't noticed that he'd been using his middle finger to scroll through the pages of his phone, but now he held it up for me to see very clearly.

The rain had softened the ground and whatever he'd been doing last night softened his senses so I was standing right next to him when I spoke. "I'm sorry, I missed that last answer. Could you repeat it for me?"

I had to give him credit. He had no fear of the unknown

stranger who was now standing and smoking on his porch. Just like before, he raised the offending digit in my direction.

The crunching noise it made in my hand was quite satisfying indeed.

Chapter 35

Like most vacationers who don't have the wisdom of experience, their kitchen was lacking in what most people take for granted. Best I could do was fill a plastic tumbler advertising one of Key West's classier establishments with ice and encourage him to stick his finger in there.

"Look on the bright side. You have nine more of those to ignore your vacation with. Now, where was I?"

He was no less happy that I had entered his life but at least he was smart enough to play along. "You said you had a couple of questions to ask me."

"How long you been here?"

"Got in Saturday, just around noon."

"Meet any of your neighbors?"

"Not more than to just introduce us and wave when we pass them."

"Any of them seem stranger than the rest?"

"I don't follow."

"Any of them look like they don't belong here?"

Just then a woman came walking out wearing what passed as pajamas these days. "Man my head is killing me." She slouched into a chair at the table, spilling her coffee. "I don't know how I'm going to survive two more days of this."

We both looked at her, but she was still trying to wake up and not the least bit aware of what was going on. "Saw one guy in a suit coming and going."

Bingo. "Where were they coming and going from?"

He gestured down the sidewalk. "Somewhere in that direction. Never saw which one, just on the sidewalk."

"Last question. You remember the last time you saw them?"

The girl finally sensed we were talking about something other than how fucked up we got last night. "What are you talking about?"

"Trying to surprise a couple of old friends. So, when was it?"

"I don't really remember." But the girl did.

"You mean the suits? Monday morning. A couple of us wanted to stay up all night. It was just about sunrise when they came up and headed to their condo. Five minutes later they came back with their luggage, and that was it."

"Thanks." I certainly didn't expect them to still be here, but it was nice to have some confirmation. "You all enjoy the rest of your vacation."

I headed down the sidewalk to see what I could see, just in time to hear the girl finally ask "Who was that, and what did he do to your finger?"

Thanks to Scooter's boat, I at least knew what I shouldn't be looking for here: anything out of place. Finding the condo prime suspects one and two had called home was a simple process of elimination. Only one condo did not have the tell-tale sign of habitation that a full recycling bin can bring to a place. Unfortunately what it did have was a stream of people moving in for a new vacation.

A quick inventory of what I was wearing convinced me I could look the part of a clueless tourist long enough to get the answers I needed. People have told me that you can catch more flies with honey than you do with shit. That busted finger qualified as shit, so I figured I should see how sweet I could be.

"Excuse me," I asked with a big enough smile as the man of the house came back out. He looked like he might struggle on an episode of "Are You Smarter Than A 5th Grader" but I wasn't looking for a Rhodes Scholar. Besides, his smile matched mine for wattage and I was sure he would be as sunny as my last friend had been sullen.

"Dave Lang," he said, his hand shooting right out for a handshake that he wouldn't say no to. I hadn't even considered a fake name, so I fell back on what I hoped would be the truth: I was never going to see this yokel again.

"Richard Lockhart," as my hand met his. "My fiancé and I are down here for a few days and I was thinking about coming back for a bit longer. Can you tell me about renting here?"

"Piece of cake. I just did a couple different searches for vacation rentals and condo rentals, and looked up some reviews online. Convenient to everything downtown and much cheaper than a hotel."

"How long do you have to rent it for?"

"One week, but we got lucky. Seems like the people who had it before us left early. The landlord called us and wanted to know if we wanted to come down early."

"More time in paradise, who could say no?" My laughter masked the fact that I'm sure it had been pretty thoroughly cleaned, but at least it confirmed this had been theirs. "Don't suppose you happen to know the name of this particular landlord."

"Honey?"

He turned his head back and called into the kitchen. From inside I heard a response just as saccharine as I expected. "Yes dear?"

"Do you have the paperwork handy? Seems we got someone who likes where we're staying."

Almost immediately a woman walked out who looked every inch of a Midwestern wife and mom. "Here you go. First time in Key West?"

"First time looking to rent here." Rule number one of lying is do as little of it as possible. Not because it's unethical, but it means there's that much less to remember later. I made the motions of looking for a pen and paper, long enough for them to know I didn't have either, and Dave ripped the top of the page off with the name and number I needed. "Thanks folks. I sure do appreciate this info." Always leave them wanting more as I stepped off the porch. "Hope you enjoy your vacation!"

"Thanks! And good luck with your wedding."

I smiled out of reflex before I even remembered I mentioned a fiancé. The second thing I remembered right away that going back the way I'd come would probably be a bad thing, so I kept going in the direction I'd first been headed. This name would come in handy, but there was someone else I had to meet up with, just to confirm that I'd missed something before.

Chapter 36

I was happy to finally see a slightly more familiar face that morning when I made the trip back to the coroner's office. He seemed a little confused to find me visiting, and me asking him how he was feeling only confused him more.

"I feel fine. Why do you ask?"

"Your replacement said they were covering for you because you were out sick."

"That's strange. She knew I was on vacation."

Apparently it was about to get even stranger. "She?"

"Dr. Joyce Kneeland."

"I'm not gonna lie Doc. I can't clearly remember the name, but he sure didn't look like a Joyce."

"Maybe she got sick and they sent someone else to cover her. Still." His voice trailed off as he began fumbling around his desk and looking through files.

"Still what?"

He remained quiet as he completed his search. I only knew him socially, and it's hard to tell how meticulous a person is when they're out having a good time. It became apparent he wanted to be sure he knew what he was talking about before he answered.

"There are no files, no documentation, no nothing of anything happening while I was gone. Which I'm guessing something did because I'm also guessing you're not just here on a social call."

"Wish that I were. You're telling me you got a body here and no paperwork to go along with it?"

"No. What I'm saying is that I don't have a body at all."

Needless to say, this caught me off guard. "There's got to be a body. I found it, I called the police, I even came down here and looked at him after he'd been sliced up for his autopsy."

He sat up a little more rigidly in his chair. "Why would he show that to you?"

Even on a laid back island some people are more straight laced than others. I didn't think he was going to be pleased to hear my story, but I didn't have any better ideas coming to mind. "The police Chief specifically asked me to handle the investigation."

I was right. His eyes popped in their sockets. "Has Chief Williams lost his mind?"

"Actually no. More like he lost his job."

"What?!"

"Look, it was kind of a busy week while you were gone." My attempt at lightening the situation was not appreciated and I quickly jumped back to the facts. "The new Chief and I worked together many years ago, and I guess he thought I'd be the best guy for the job."

"And you agreed?"

"Not at first, but he made some pretty persuasive arguments."

He leaned back in his chair, not at all happy with what was going on and who (meaning me) he thought was responsible for it. "You're telling me a person dies, you found the body, somehow it became your 'case', for lack of a better term, and now the body, the coroner and the paperwork are all missing?"

"Sounds about right."

"Pretty murky waters we're in here, ethically."

"Yeah, but as long as we're still treading water."

He leaned back in. "Dick, I don't even like to stick my toe in these waters, but thanks to my kids burning desire for all things Harry Potter, I seem to find my office flooding with it." He turned to his computer. "Let's start with the name of the coroner. Maybe we can track him down at least." When I didn't say anything he returned his vision to me. "Oh right. You don't remember his name."

It wouldn't do me much good to say no, out loud, so I kept my mouth shut.

"Suddenly I feel the water getting deeper. How about the dead body? You got a name for him?"

He was making me feel like a kid called before the principal, and like any kid who wanted to get out of being punished, I was happy to answer what questions I could. "Scooter. And he was most assuredly dead, trust me."

"Scooter? That crusty old bastard who's always at Barnacle Bob's? Who'd want to kill him?"

"Surprisingly a lot of people."

"Which I'm guessing means you have a suspect."

"That's where it gets murky again." I explained to him how Scooter had been tied up underwater, the antifreeze pumped into his veins and the fishing weights pumped into his stomach. By the time I got to the part of being drowned in fresh water and found in salt water I could tell he would have done anything to still be on vacation and never come back.

He took another minute of silence before he stood up and grabbed his keys off his desk. "C'mon. I might as well meet the new boss. Hopefully he'll know more than you. God knows he certainly couldn't know any less."

"I'll meet you there. My boat's tied off in the mangroves."

"And that's where it's going to stay. I'm not wasting any more time on this than has already been wasted."

Terry

Chapter 37

Maybe getting him out of that room full of death finally made him talkative. On the drive back into town he explained to me how almost useless his position as coroner of Monroe County was.

"Do you know how many people who die here each year need my signature?"

"All of them?"

"That's not how it works. Guess again."

"I've got no idea."

"Neither do I, because I've never learned to count that low."

"I thought everyone who dies needs a death certificate."

"Everyone does. And most of them get theirs signed by the doctor that watched them die of natural causes. I don't even realize most people die in this county until I read about it in the paper. I investigate maybe 60, maybe 80 deaths a year, two thirds of which happen during the first four months of the year."

"Tourists?"

"That's the polite word for them."

"If the whole county is yours, why live all the way down here?"

He shot me a look from the corner of his eye. "Do you want to live in Marathon?" Point taken. "The thing that confuses me."

I cut him off. "You mean more than the amateur detective, missing corpse and extra coroner?"

"Is who transferred the phone call where."

"What do you mean?"

"The coroner covering my vacation – in theory, Dr. Kneeland – isn't like a substitute teacher who comes down and sits in my office. She was working full time in Miami-Dade County."

"How many coroners do they have?"

"Not enough. Couple dozen maybe. Remember, when you're the Medicare fraud capital of the world, lots of people die for no good reason. The officer who took the body would have called my office and been transferred up to Miami and put in touch with Joyce."

"Then what? Wait for her?"

"Key West cops don't deliver beyond city limits. Protocol would have at least one officer bring the body to the morgue and wait with it until the coroner arrived and signed off on delivery, in effect taking ownership."

"And protocol says that, body or not, there would at least have been a copy of the transfer sheet in your office."

He smiled and nodded. "Now you see why I'm confused."

Chapter 38

For someone who claimed to be chronically underemployed he still had a reserved spot at the police station. He let me lead the way and I caught the Chief's eye as he was finishing up a phone call.

"Dick, come on in and bring your friend."

"He's your friend too, but I don't know for how much longer."

"That's an odd way form of introduction."

He reached across the desk to shake the Chief's hand. "I'm Dr. Henry Santacrose, Monroe County medical examiner."

The Chief hastily stood up and took his hand. "Hello Doc. It's an honor to meet you. Still haven't had the time to make the rounds and introduce myself to everyone. Judging by the company you keep, you must be here about Scooter."

"I would be, if there was a Scooter to be here about."

"Come again?"

The Chief was about to get blindsided, and although there was a substantial part of me that would enjoy seeing it happen, I knew that like it or not, I was as caught up in this shit storm as he was. The doc's image of the murky water came back to me, and if I didn't want to go under I needed to catch the Chief up quick.

"I stopped by to see if Scooter had any defensive wounds on him, something I hadn't thought to look for before, but when I got to the morgue Scooter was missing. As was the mystery coroner and any evidence either one of them had been here at all."

"The mystery coroner?"

"Dr. Joyce Kneeland was supposed to cover my vacation," the doc said, "but according to Dick that wasn't who handled the autopsy."

"No, no it wasn't." He sank back into his chair, a man suddenly on the verge of collapse but still fighting to win. "Dr. Kneeland was unavailable, if I remember right."

"Out sick," I offered.

"Right, so doctor...doctor...shit, it was right on the tip of my tongue. He called me about an hour after you left him." He turned to me with a look in his eye I'd seen from a hundred different men in a thousand separate situations. I was to shut up until I was asked a direct question. "Turns out there were other chemicals in his blood that he couldn't identify, so he wanted to take the body back up to Miami and their more advanced laboratory."

"There would have been some documentation about the body going from one county to another."

"That's what I asked him, but he said that since he was the coroner of record and employed by Miami-Dade County it wouldn't be an issue. I pressed him, because this was obviously the victim of a crime, but he explained that was actually the reason for the justification." My eyebrow instinctively shot up as I tried to make sense of his last words. He knew he was in danger of losing it, so he decided it was time for a little misdirection. "Of course, much of this hassle would have been avoided if Dick here wasn't such a Luddite and would consent to having a phone. Isn't that right?"

There was my cue. "Well you know how it is. Gone are the days when I used to enjoy someone reaching out to touch me."

"I don't think you have to worry much about that, phone or no phone." He got up from the desk and walked towards the doc at just the right angle to let him know he could leave now. "I'm sorry for all this miscommunication. And I know I have that, what did you call him Dick, the mystery coroner?"

"That's him."

"I know I have his name around here somewhere. I'll get it to you and the two of you can compare notes or switch files or whatever else you have to do." The Chief has a laugh that I'm sure he learned in a school you've never heard of. It was almost hypnotic in the way it defused situations and distracted people. "I've spent a lifetime in government service, but this is my first time running a police department, so I'm still learning all of the protocol."

The doc shot a look in my direction. "Seems like you might be making some of it up as you go along."

He just kept on laughing. "It does seem that way, doesn't it? Well, once again I'm glad to have finally met you, and I'll get you that name." He even patted him on the back like the two of them were old friends. There was no way the doc could be anything but more confused, and yet he no longer seemed to care.

The Chief stood in the doorway until the doc was out of the building. When it had been the three of us the door had stayed open. Now that our trio had become a duo, he shut it and crossed back to his desk.

"How much of that was true?" I asked him.

"How much of it sounded true?"

"None of it."

"Even less than that."

"What are you going to do about the coroner?"

He leaned back and cradled his head in his hands. "I'll

find someone up north to take the call. He's probably half ticked because it would have been something exciting for a change, but if we can sell it to him as something far less sinister than it appears, hopefully he'll lose interest."

"Shouldn't be a problem. We seem to be losing everything else. The phone call can placate Henry, but seriously, who the fuck has Scooter right now?"

"I thought that might make you happy."

"Whaddya mean?"

"No body, nothing left for you to worry about."

Had that been the case 72 hours ago I would have agreed with him, but he was right. I couldn't let something like this go; no matter what I thought of the guy while he was living, now I was too invested in finding out why he was dead.

"Well, now I guess the body count has doubled. Need to find Scooter and the mystery coroner."

"Speaking of which, I actually did hear from your coroner friend the other day. He was looking for you."

"He already found me." I told him about his final visit to the boat right before he left town. The Chief seemed less interested in the water than I would have thought.

"Why didn't he return your bag then?"

"What bag?"

"The one you left at the morgue when you looked at the body."

"I didn't have a bag with me."

"Well he says you did. It's down at the evidence room."

I got up to leave but I couldn't resist asking him again.

"Why me Chief?"

He looked so lost that I figured he wasn't going to answer me but he finally did. "Because I knew. I knew something like this was going to happen. I knew that none of it made sense, and I needed someone who understood that things didn't have to make sense in order to have an answer. I just didn't know it was going to get this deep."

"That's why the Coast Guard didn't get involved. You never called them."

He just shook his head. Knowing what I knew, or at least thought might be the case, he might have actually saved us a world of problems by not reaching out to them

I realized I had more questions than that, but now wasn't the time to ask them, so I shut the door behind me and went to claim my door prize. It took the sergeant a few minutes of looking before he realized nobody had put it away. "Why the fuck would they leave it right here?" And then he tried to pick it up.

"Jesus fuck, that must weigh a ton."

It was an old army backpack, and I had a terrifying sense of déjà vu. I had a bag just like it in college, so in a sense it was my bag, whether I wanted it or not.

"Ain't you going to look to see if it's all there?"

"Don't have to," I said as I swung it on my back. Sure enough the weight shifted and I could tell exactly what it was.

Fifty pounds of fucking fishing weights.

Chapter 39

Every step I took filled me with a conviction to just throw the bag away, but there had to be a reason he thought I should have it. As I stumbled towards the dinghy dock I tried to figure out what those reasons could be.

1) He thought Scooter and I were friends. Not knowing either of us from Adam, and here I was being the one investigating the murder, maybe he thought we had a connection, used to go fishing together, even though I told him I had no interest, and I wouldn't want his old fishing equipment, now extra clean after sitting in his stomach acid.

2) He thought that it could serve as some sort of payment for being a good citizen and looking into the murder. I'm not sure what the market value of fifty pounds of lead is these days, but I was pretty sure it wouldn't cover the cost of the chiropractic visit I was going to need after humping this bag a dozen blocks across the island.

3) He thought it would be funny. I mean, if this guy is silly/dumb enough to impersonate a coroner and steal a body, who knows what else he does to get his rocks off?

And that was the crux of it. I had to accept that this guy had been a fake, because of all the things he didn't think about: he didn't think that these weights could be considered evidence (although at least now that they were in my possession my earlier fingering of them wasn't so crucial), he didn't think it was important to tell the Chief that he was giving me this evidence, and he didn't think anyone was going to notice him missing with the body and come looking for him.

What was starting to bother me, besides the ridiculous weight, was something the coroner – the real one – had said about how little he actually worked. If this guy was just looking for a body to steal, why do it somewhere where the opportunity might not present itself very often? If Miami has a couple of dozen medical examiners, and they're understaffed, that seems like a far more logical place to go body snatching. Here just seemed like too much of a gamble.

It was a thought that stopped me in my tracks.

What if it hadn't been a gamble?

It's obvious that whoever wanted Scooter killed wanted him found. Otherwise he would have been shark bait. But what if once he was found, they wanted to make sure he got lost again? It seemed like they wanted to make sure people knew he had been killed purposely, but then they wanted to get him away before people learned too much about it. The ultimate message murder.

To make that happen they would need to guarantee a man on the inside, maybe even two. They learn the coroner is going on vacation and find out who is going to cover for him. Then they either find a way to keep her out of the loop, or more likely simply get someone to slip her something so she's down but not out. With her out sick, an already stressed out work place becomes more of a headache, so when the call comes to drive 150 miles and waste a day and a half, send the new guy who nobody was expecting.

Suddenly the weight on my back got a whole lot heavier. This present might just be his way of letting me know we both know what's going on. He could have driven down, picked up the body and been back in Miami that night. Instead he waited so he could explain to someone what they had done to him.

Not just someone. Me.

I said maybe two guys on the inside, didn't I?

"I knew something like this was going to happen. I just didn't know it was going to get this deep."

One of those wasted questions had been almost the same as the one he answered: "Why you Chief?" He had no business running a police department anywhere in this country, much less at the end of the road. He had done a lot of jobs over the last thirty years, only about a tenth of which were appropriate for a typical resume, and none of them had involved working with the public. He certainly knew something was going to happen. So did a bunch of somebody elses and they made sure he was here to get me involved. Hell, it's even like he knew I was going to be the one who found the body, and that thought was disturbing enough to make me stop thinking about it all together.

Pushing those thoughts out of my mind, I tried to clear my head and think about forgetting this whole thing. There was no body anymore, so as far as I wanted to be concerned, my work here was done, although I knew it wasn't that simple. Webs get built with many strings, and the more you try to work your way out of one, the more strings you find yourself getting wrapped up in. I wanted to sail away from all of this and start fresh somewhere, but two things wouldn't let that happen: me, and everybody that wanted me to be a part of this.

With all of this shit rattling around my mind, I totally forget about the much more pressing problem. When I got to the dinghy dock, that pressing problem fucked me up just as much as the rest of them had: My ride was five miles away tied up to the mangroves.

I decided to call this day officially over and drink until

none of it mattered. Luckily I was right next door to a bar.

Chapter 40

I was on my third round of drinks when Mike the Pipe came over and sat next to me. "You look like someone who spent the whole day at the track betting on the wrong horse."

"Something like that."

"Maybe you were closer to Scooter than you thought."

Maybe, but not in the way that Mike meant, and as much as I liked him I didn't feel like trying to explain it, so I just said "Maybe."

"I was harsh on him earlier, and I'm sorry for that."

"You don't have to apologize to me for that. Lots of people around here feel the same way as you, some with better reasons but most with no good reason at all."

He considered that for a moment before he spoke. "The apology isn't really for you. It's for him, and me, and I guess whatever is out there rolling our dice. I wished a man dead for something he did to me, but now that he's gone, I understand it changes nothing. It doesn't wash away my memories and it doesn't edit the past. All it does it make me feel petty and small."

"Don't. You're a good man, and you can't beat yourself up for what you felt."

"Maybe. Maybe not. But the same goes for you."

He headed back to where he'd been sitting and I drifted back into what I hadn't been able to tell him.

The manatee had been right. What hit the closest to home

about all of this were the surface similarities between Scooter and myself. Two guys, retired and living on a sailboat, not too many friends and even fewer family members. I hoped I was slightly more well-liked than he had been; normally I wouldn't be worried about that, but if it had been his ability to piss people off that led to his death then maybe it was something to consider. Even more than the similarities, what was really sticking in my craw were the differences.

A man doesn't need to litter his boat with hidden compartments if he doesn't have secrets hidden in the shadows. Scooter almost seemed like someone who had nothing to hide. In life, everybody's got something they don't like to talk about. Maybe it's as benign as a third nipple or a lousy golf handicap, or maybe it's the dark weight of a child that was lost or a parent that wasn't. Every day, all over the world, people live their lives, the whole time bargaining with this secret and how they're going to deal with it.

I looked around the bar, taking in the faces, and I wondered what secret each of these people had. Who went home and beat their spouse, and who was here so they wouldn't be home for the beating? Whose skeleton in the closet was actually a body in a landfill? Who smiled in public because they cried in private? And who had twenty-five years of wondering if the choices they made and the family they walked out on had been worth it? Who was sitting here, alone, wondering if the secrets they had amassed during that quarter of a century were now slipping out through the cracks, and one day those shadows, the same ones that haunted his sleep and drove him to find old ways in order to have some new solutions, would show up at his boat someday, just before sunset, looking for retribution?

I spent another...hour? Two? Long enough for the day time entertainment to finish and Caffeine Carl to set up and get started, for day to become night and for most of the crowd to change. I took in everyone, one face at a time, and I tallied my score against what I imagined theirs to be. I invented names, made up pasts, pushed my imagination, and I could still not conjure a life for anyone that exceeded my own. I wish I could say it frightened me, but the truth was I found some comfort in it. If nothing else I always knew who I was and what I had done. It wasn't pride. It was merely acceptance.

A pat on my back broke my concentration. Mike said nothing as he shuffled home for the night, but his touch said it all: 'Lighten the fuck up. It's just life, and none of us make it out alive anyway.' Watching him leave somehow did the trick and I thought I felt my spirits rise.

Carl was jamming with blues you could use, as they used to say, and it reminded me of better days. Funny how music built on sadness can make you feel better, but when it's played well in the right environment it's something magical. The last of the shit weather had drifted away and the clouds left behind were frightening shades of purples, soaked up in the last of the sunset and being invested by the night. The air was thick with moisture, but in a cool invasive manner, and the music hung in it, becoming something you felt in your body as much as heard through your ears. I finally found myself feeling some measure of uneasy peace for the first time this week, and I really thought it might be able to stay with me for a while. It took about fifteen seconds to be proven wrong.

There was a rising of voices to my left, punctuated by a "Son of a bitch" loud enough to draw everyone's attention. I turned to see my BFF from Miami looking awfully pissed off.

"What the fuck, he didn't pay? That old man said he was buying us drinks and then stuck us with the bill? Fuck that shit."

Spending a lot of drunken time in the dark recesses of your mind apparently messes with your sense of humor, because somehow I found this funny and laughed out loud. Sunny Crocket heard this, saw me, and decided I was to blame for everything.

"You think this is funny, fuckface?" (Fuckface? It was seventh grade all over again.) "You'll be laughing through a wired jaw if you don't shut the fuck up."

He was walking towards me as he was talking, and like any good dick his two friends followed him like the nuts they were. This image was just as humorous as him thinking Mike had stuck them with the bill and I kept laughing.

"You got about ten seconds to explain yourself before I lose my patience on you." By now he was right in my face, and although I doubted it would work, I tried to clarify the situation without standing up.

"Nobody stuck you with nothing. Mike comes back every morning and pays then."

"No bar is going to fucking hold a tab all night."

"Maybe not for an asshole like you, but they do it for Mike all the time. Go ahead, ask the bartender."

I could see one of his goons thought that would be the sensible thing to do, but I could also see that Prince Asshole here hadn't done a sensible thing in probably a dozen years. "I'm not talking to a bartender. I'm talking to you fuckface, and you're about down to two seconds before I flatten you."

Yup, it was seventh grade all over again. One night after a junior high dance, I had gotten into my first fight, right in front of a Dairy Queen. The weather here was much warmer, and the treats were for an adult clientele, but it looked like it was going to happen all over again.

I believe enough in myself to think that I'm an advanced person who doesn't have to resort to physical violence. Many times that has been the case. But I also know that sometimes the best thing to do is to step out of the rational mind for a while. Opposable thumbs notwithstanding, we are all still animals, and when the fight or flight instinct kicks in, it feels damn good to stand your ground. I put down my beer, slid out from the stool, and stood in front of him.

"Two, one, zero. So, now what are you going to do?"

I could tell that wasn't the response he expected. I couldn't figure out if he expected me to say something as douchey as he had, or to just sit there and apologize. Apparently neither could he because he didn't say anything, so I figured I should speak for both of us.

"I'm going to make a suggestion to you, Larry and Curly here. I'm going to suggest you walk out of this bar and go to wherever you are calling home on this vacation. Do not pass go, do not collect two hundred dollars, and most certainly do not hesitate. Because I am having a supremely shitty week, and I am not the person you want to be fucking with right now."

My words were soft and direct, and with enough charge in them that the people around us felt the atmosphere change. From the corner of my eyes I could see them shifting, backing away from the action but staying close enough to witness it. I knew I could count on a few of them if it got that far, but I hoped that it wouldn't. To guarantee that I could keep it contained, I needed to make sure I knew what I was up against.

One of his henchmen was just drinking a beer, like he had

been here a hundred times before, and all that happened on ninety nine of those occasions was a lot of hot air. His buddy however looked a lot more concerned, a little more scared and a whole lot nervous. He was starting to twitch a little bit. Spastic people are unpredictable in a fight and I'd have to keep an eye on him. Meanwhile, Captain Toe Cheese proved to be as stupid as his haircut.

"Listen you drunk fucker. You've done nothing but piss me off since I first saw you. I've been letting it slide, but now that you think you can stand up to me, it's time I knocked you down a peg or two."

"Trust me, I really hope you try. It's been a while since I've had to slap a bitch around, and you're making my slapping hand real itchy." I could feel the blood moving faster through my veins, and I knew I was crossing the line. I hate to say it, but there are times that blood wants blood and won't be satisfied with anything less.

"If anyone's the bitch, it's you. Complete with your bitch purse. Is that what you're going to do? Hit me with your purse?" He pushed at it with his foot, and it pleased me to realize he hadn't put enough pressure on it to discover how heavy it was.

"You should hope that I do. It's so heavy that it would knock you the fuck out in one swing. Pussy like you probably couldn't even lift it."

He smiled the crooked grin of someone who trusted too much in what he lifted in the gym and not enough in the rest of the world. "Maybe it's too heavy for a bitch like you, but let me show you how."

Someday I want to meet this guy's parents, so I can thank them for raising a son as dumb as they did. Sure enough Admiral Asshole started to slowly reach down for the bag. He was moving very deliberately, his eyes fixed directly on mine, but I knew his intention. As soon as he had it in his hand he was going to switch to full speed and bring it straight up into my body. No matter where he made contact it would be enough to distract me, and him and his boys would have the advantage.

His hand was about an inch from the handle, and I said a prayer of thanksgiving.

This was going to be sweet.

Chapter 41

When you drop something breakable, afterwards you can't understand how you didn't have time to catch it. It seems like it was falling forever. You have time to see the coffee spilling out, time to see the handle just beyond your reach, but ultimately only time enough to watch it shatter. Of course it has nothing to do with time slowing down. It's simply your mind enhancing your awareness while it tries to process everything and time becomes elastic. How else do you explain your life flashing before your eyes in the second before you die?

As soon as Major Misfit touched the bag he went for his move and almost dislocated his shoulder. I don't know what he thought I was carrying – feathers? Bubble wrap? – but he certainly wasn't expecting lead weights. I began to move on him and saw two things, one that made me happy and the other than almost made me shit.

Buddy Budweiser was making my life easy by keeping his bottle right up in front of his mouth, but his friend, Sister Spastic, wasn't suffering from a nervous tic. His hands had been dancing around his waistband because that was where his gun was. Knowing this, I should have sent the lead asshole into him, but my weight was already shifting so I was going to have to work fast.

Sergeant Shithead grunted once when his arm locked up trying to lift the bag. His second grunt, courtesy of my right knee catching him flush on his jaw, was both much louder and vastly muffled. His third noise was a howl of pain. He was off balance enough so the force of my blow sent him spiraling around. By the time I stepped through him he was on his knees, cradling his jaw and screaming in agony.

Once my feet were settled, I was in a southpaw stance and came out with an open handed straight jab. It landed squarely on the bottom of the bottle and drove it straight through his mouth. You might think glass would be more fragile than enamel. You would be wrong, but if you were in the bar that night I would forgive you for being mistaken. It turns out the sound of shattering glass is very similar to that of smashing teeth. Both however sound much different from that of a semi-conscious body hitting the ground.

By now the third amigo had the gun drawn and pointed in my direction. His finger was quick but his aim was off. I was close enough to feel the muzzle flash on my neck and still the bullet went whistling past me. I didn't give him any time to improve his aim. I grabbed his arm and twisted down while his finger kept working the trigger. The second bullet buried itself in the ground and the third one did the same into his Achilles. With more pressing issues on his mind he let the gun go. I caught it on the fly.

My new best friend was still holding his face and screaming obscenities, so I was surprised he was able to hear me cocking the hammer. Maybe that wasn't what got his attention and shut him the hell up though.

Maybe it was feeling the warm barrel of a gun on his temple.

Chapter 42

Funny thing about gun shots in a crowded bar: they tend to get people's attention. Carl and the band screeched to a halt like a needle on a record, and after a chorus of screams punctuated by furniture hitting the ground, the only noises left were Achilles screaming about his heel, Lieutenant Loser whimpering about his jaw, and a very excited patois of a kitchen full of Haitians.

"Everyone all right in there, Jean?" (No, I don't know any of the cooks personally, but with six of them back there my odds were good that at least one of them was named Jean. If you don't like my stereotyping, take it up with Sean Penn.)

"We fine, but we gonna need a new fryer."

I lowered my voice and moved around my Miami friend, lining the gun up so it was directly between his eyes. "Looks like it's your lucky day and nobody is going to drop a little hoodoo Voodoo curse on you today. (Once again, call Sean.) "Care to keep playing press your luck?"

His whimpering was affecting his speech. "Wha...what...what do you mean?"

"Your friend shot at me from about six inches away and missed." I moved the gun back that same distance. "Do you want to see if I'm as bad a shot as he is?"

The whimper won out but after a few seconds I heard another noise: the sound of urine running down his legs and hitting the gravel.

A new noise came from behind the bar as the phone

started to ring. "It's okay," I said to whoever was still back there. "You can answer that."

"Hello, Barnacle Bob's." The bartender spoke timidly into the phone. "Hold on, I'll check." She got marginally louder. "Excuse me, but are you Richard Lockhart?"

"Yes I am."

"It's for you." She tried to stay as far away as possible while handing me the phone. I switched hands and took the phone, and she quickly scampered back to the far side of the bar.

"Hello Chief."

"Why did I know you'd be at the center of the gunfire?"

"I was bored with the turtle races."

"What's going on?"

"Well, you know me, just making friends and influencing people."

"Mmm-hmmm. Let me talk to the head asshole in charge."

I handed the phone down to my BFF. "He wants to talk to you. Be nice. It's the Chief of police."

He dry swallowed a couple of times. "Hello?"

"What's your name?"

"Peter."

"Peter what?"

"Peter...Uh...Peter..."

"Peter Pisspants," I volunteered. I figured if we were going back to seventh grade with fuckface, why not go back even a few grades earlier? His instinct was to shoot me a look. Mine was to press the gun back against his forehead. The Chief's was to keep talking.

"Maybe you can tell me why you pissed yourself."

"This guy is holding a gun to my head."

"Uh-huh. And is it his gun?"

"No, um, no sir."

"I see. Whose gun is it?"

"My...my friend's."

"And what is your friend doing now?"

"He's...uh...he's trying to stop the bleeding, and the other one"

The Chief cut him off. "Other one? Jesus how many of you are there?"

"Three."

"Three, huh? Three of you, you probably had the jump, and you still lost?"

"Yes."

"So back to the third one. What's he doing?"

"Trying to find his teeth, I think."

"Mmm-hmmm. Peter, I'm going to go out on a limb and guess you're not from around here."

"No sir. Miami."

"Figures. Okay, so Peter, here's the deal. The man holding the gun is possibly one of my least favorite people in the world, but I owe him a few favors. Now, I could give him those favors by letting him finish off what you started. Would you like that?"

He started to tremble. "No sir."

"Neither would I. That's far too much paperwork for me to handle, and I'd rather cash those favors in for something important. So we're going to make a deal. I'm going to give you a ten minute head start. If you're not there, or anywhere on the island, when those ten minutes are up, then I won't arrest you for assault, weapons possession, etc., etc. Sound good?"

"Off the island, sir?"

"Yup."

"But...but we won't have time to pack."

"What's more important Peter? Your Dolce and Gabana banana hammocks or your freedom?"

"Our wives are not with us. We won't have time to find them."

"They'll probably enjoy their vacation more that way. Clock is ticking Peter. Now hand the phone back to my friend."

I took it back from him. "Yes?"

"Don't be there when we show up." He didn't even give me time to say "of course not" before he hung up. I put the phone down on the bar and looked at my friend.

"I guess we each have our orders." I put the hammer down and slid the gun into my shorts. He collapsed onto the ground and started sobbing while I finished my beer. "I guess I'm ready for my check." The same timid bartender came back down. I hadn't seen her before tonight. "I hope this isn't your first shift."

"Third."

"Nice to meet you. I'm Richard Lockhart, as you know, but my friends call me Tricky Dick."

"Nice to meet you," though I'm not sure she meant it. "I'm Abby."

I placed a few bills on the bar top before I struggled getting the backpack on. "I'm usually not this much of an attention getter. Have a nice night."

I walked by the survivors as they struggled to their feet. My head actually felt clear and I had a peaceful energy coursing through my veins. Like I said, sometimes blood needs blood.

Of course the one problem it didn't solve was my lack of transportation. Even without fifty pounds of dead weight on my back, being out in public was probably not a good idea. That was when I saw a figure emerging from the shadows of the dock. Problem solved.

"My angel in black."

"Buy me a drink sailor?"

"Not tonight. Long story."

"Does it have anything to do with the gun shots?"

"I'll explain on the way back to your boat."

"Don't you have your dinghy?"

"Not tonight. Long story. I'll explain on the way back to your boat."

"Man of mystery. I like it."

I had nothing to say to that. Too many mysteries, too little time.

Chapter 43

She made us some drinks while I gave her the recap of my night's activities. I was sure to mention my earlier entanglements with this particular gentleman, but studiously avoided any mention of the backpack, the coroner and the lack of a dead body.

"But enough of my shop talk. How was Miami for you?"

"Just another day at the office. I did get an opportunity I wanted to run by you."

"Yeah? What's that?"

"They need me to go to Bimini to write up a photo shoot, interview a couple of models, fun stuff like that."

"And they need someone to help them get into their skimpy outfits?"

"Hardly. They have plenty of people for that. What I need is someone to help me crew."

"Crew what?"

"My boat." She settled in next to me. "The shoot doesn't start until Monday, which gives us plenty of time to sail out there."

"You're forgetting that I have previous entanglements here."

"If the Chief wanted to talk to you about the shooting tonight he already would have."

"Well, there's that, plus the little pressing matter of a dead body."

She looked at me and her eyes picked up what little light

was in the night. "Have you officially been made a member of the force?"

"No, but..." I let my voice trail off, and she was smart enough to know what I meant by it. As strange as the whole case had gotten, far stranger than she was even aware of, I still felt that sense of duty to find out what had happened. Truth was I was farther out of my element than ever before. The trail was getting stretched out far beyond the island, and that might force me to follow it to places I didn't want to go. Which was much like what she was asking me to do, and that led to the next conversation.

"Look, I haven't been completely open with you about my past."

"Are you a wanted man?"

Shit, she didn't give me a whole lot of wiggle room. "Not in what you would think of as the conventional, poster in the post office, sort of sense."

She sat up quickly. "You're not joking?"

I stood to pace. If you think remembering what I had done in my life was uncomfortable, imagine how it felt trying to explain it to someone, especially when there was so little that you could actually say. Before I could find words she continued to speak. "Tell me you're not responsible for doing bad things to people."

"That's just it. Good and bad are matters of perspective."

I could feel her grow a little icier. "Only when you are trying to justify doing bad things and making them seem good."

It was a mistake. All of it. I knew it, had known it from the start. I should have just handed her back her panties, thanked her for an unforgettable time I had already forgotten, and gone back to my solitary life. "I guess it doesn't matter what I say next then."

"Say this: If I go to Bimini, someone is going to shoot me and everybody I might be with."

"Probably not. There are only a few people who ever wanted me dead in the first place, and based on their lifestyle choices I've probably outlived them. Plus, I've been there enough to know we can sneak in and out without anyone knowing I'm there."

"But you still don't want to go."

"It's a chance I don't know I want to take. For your benefit as much as mine." I tried to lighten the situation by changing the subject, however slightly. "Besides, I don't know the first thing about crewing a sailboat."

"How can you not? You live on one."

"I dropped that anchor two and a half years ago and haven't moved it since."

"What if a storm comes?"

"Hope for the best." I settled back in next to her. "How long you going to be gone?"

"Eight or nine days. Truth is I can make the sail on my own. I was just hoping to have a cabin boy for the trip."

"Sorry."

She nestled into my shoulder and was silent for a minute. "Man of mystery."

"Sorry?"

"There's just so much of you I don't know. I guess that's the price a person pays for living down here."

"Don't feel so bad. There's a lot about you I don't know."

"Including my name."

How did she know that? "How do you know that?"

"We talked about it before, nitwit. Besides, you're a guy. If you can't remember sleeping with me that first time, you certainly aren't going to remember my name. But you're too dumbly proud to ask me now."

"Well, now that you've called me out about it, I'm not."

"Rachel."

"Pleased to meet you Rachel. Named after anyone in particular?"

"Quite the opposite."

"Huh?"

She leaned forward, as if she needed to get closer in order to see all the facts of the story. "When my parents discovered I was going to be a girl, they started to think of names. But they wanted to make sure it was a name that didn't have a past for either one of them. It couldn't be the name of an ex-girlfriend of my dad's or an old roommate of my mom. She explained it to me that eventually, everybody reminds you of somebody. They knew that would happen to me, that I would behave or look like someone they knew, and they didn't want to handicap that process by naming me after somebody one of them already had a past with. Eventually they stumbled on the name Rachel and both of them realized it would work."

"That's certainly one of the stranger ways of naming a child."

She crossed over to the bar, still lost in the memory of her childhood. "My parents had several unconventional methods when it came to raising their children." She picked up the bottle but didn't refill her glass. "C'mon. I'm tired from my trip, and you must be exhausted from your duties as the island ambassador."

I was actually feeling some of the adrenaline still, but when she turned back to face me, I could see that she had let the memories slip away and my adrenaline might be a little useful.

"You're going to try and convince me to change my mind."

"Maybe. Or maybe I'll just Shanghai you." She came back to me and as she filled my drink with one hand she unzipped her dress with the other. Her perfect skin glowed in the dusky night, and the matching black bra and panties might have been the sexiest outfit I ever saw. She leaned in but instead of kissing me she pressed her lips to my ear. "Everybody reminds me of somebody, but you don't remind me of anybody. Why is that?" She stood back up and turned for the cabin hatch. "Is that because there's nobody like you in the world?"

Chapter 44

It wasn't the sound of a passing boat but the strange effect of its wake that woke me up. I couldn't figure out why the boat was rocking the way it was. It was more of an up and down motion and not the side to side I had gotten used to over the years from riding a wave broadside. I was just about to sit up and investigate when I felt something more than just motion. I laid back and enjoyed this most personal way of being woken up.

When she finished she gave me a warm kiss before getting out of bed. I watched her do a perfunctory job of cleaning up before dressing to go top side. Even her bathing suit was black. Made no sense.

It was no longer a strange bed to wake up in, naked or not, but I knew I couldn't spend all morning lying in her sheets. She had to be making waves soon in order to sail out with the tide, and I had a dinghy to track down. Her cleaning had included folding my clothes, so I slipped into my shorts and was fumbling with my shirt while walking up the stairs.

She handed me a cup of coffee as I emerged, my eyes straining in the daylight. "The offer still stands," she said. "It would be fun to have some company, and even more fun if that company was you. Plus, even though Bimini is so close, the Coast Guard recommends going with a sailing buddy."

"And your boss would be okay with you showing up with a stranger."

She acted as if she was thinking about that. "My boss is okay with me taking my time to sail there. I'm sure he'd be okay with me bringing a cabin boy, although I suspect he would prefer I not bring one that might get us all shot."

I felt bad that I had said as much as I had, and felt worse that I hadn't been able to say more. It was a surprisingly tempting offer, potential death wish notwithstanding. It was not unlike what I had been thinking yesterday, and for the first time all week I didn't get spooked by seeing how it might be connected. There had been too many strange coincidences in my life lately, and meeting her had been one of them. Getting away with her, separating her from the rest of them, might help me to get a better feel for who she is and make sure that she wasn't part of a bigger issue. The fact that she was comfortable with me accompanying her meant meeting her had probably been just that: a chance meeting in the middle of a downpour. I knew from personal experience that a job could be a front, but there is a world of difference between telling people you have a particular job only to then be vague about the details and inviting a plus one to come along with you. Of course, the temptation of the trip was tempered by one other thing.

"The Chief might still want to talk to me about last night." He had given his assurances over the phone, but gunplay and bleeding tourists have a way of getting noticed. "I probably should stick around for a while."

"It's not like you're running away. Think of it as a planned vacation, and you can give your witness statement when you get back."

"I was a little more than just a witness."

"Did you pull the trigger?"

"No, but I did break one guy's face and separate another from several of his teeth."

She dismissed me with a wave of her hand. "Tomayto, tomahto. Take the dinghy, go find yours and make up your mind. I'm leaving in an hour, so you better be back by then, if for no other reason to return my boat. But," and her voice became a coo, "if you come with me, I promise you a surprise."

Well, the Captain had spoken, so if I wanted to be the cabin boy I was going to have to follow her directions. I hoisted up the backpack, hopped in the dinghy and set off for the fuel dock, where Smitty was paying more attention to the coffee in his right hand than he was the broom in his left.

"Tell me again how this works. I say 'how much for'?"

"And I tell you I don't do that."

"Not even for this much?"

"It would have to be at least that much."

I pulled a bill out, crumpled it up and hit him in the chest with it. "I need my dinghy brought back to my boat. Parked it over in the mangroves near the hospital. It's"

"Probably the only one there. Most people drive to the hospital, or take advantage of this thing called an ambulance."

"I don't care how young you look. Keep talking like that and you ain't going to age another day."

"Tell you what. If I find more than one I'll bring 'em all back and you can choose your favorite." I was thinking of making good on my threat when he laughed. "Flaking green paint with a refurbished Evinrude. I got it."

"Thanks. I might be gone when you bring it back so just tie it off."

"Tie it off to what? If you're gone, you're gone."

"You've seen my boat. I'm not crazy enough to take that anywhere. I'm going with a friend."

"The brunette that's two boats over from you? Nice."

"Just get my dinghy and bring it back." I pushed off and started to turn around.

"Hey!"

"Yeah?"

He had finally uncrumpled the bill. "The last guys I did a favor for paid the same way. You sure you ain't with them?"

"Promise."

"Is that why you might be going away? To try and find them?"

I don't like lying that early in the morning, but he looked like someone who was only a couple of years removed from being told by his father that his dog had not bought the farm but sent off to one and believe it.

"Something like that. Everything's a possibility, you know?" I throttled the engine so I wouldn't have to hear his reply and headed back to my boat.

Chapter 45

The bag hit the table with an audible thump. I still didn't know what I was going to do, but figured I had about thirty minutes to decide. It felt pointless to go back looking for more clues; everything that was connected with Scooter was gone except for the bird sanctuary his boat had turned into. But if the Chief wanted to talk to me about that, or the shooting, or any other shit he felt like dumping on me, it would make things easier for me to be on dry land. The more I thought about it, the more I realized that making it easy on him was the last thing I was going to do. If he wanted to talk to me, he could come out here and find me. If I was still here.

I hadn't been joking about the threats on my life if I went to Bimini, but I was also serious when I said I've probably outlived everyone who had it out for me. I may have been the cleanest person in some of the dirtiest situations in the world. That's what happened when the only contraband you specialized in was information. People would go out of their way to find out what I knew. They would pay handsomely for it, and they would believe it without a second thought. They also would want to make sure I didn't tell anyone else what I knew, so most of the time I was sharing my secrets with one foot out the door. Of course it could be hard to do that when all the doors were shut around you, and you had to have a plan B, C and D. I hadn't learned to do what I did last night by drinking tea and playing pinochle.

I stared at the bag, thinking my decision would come from it, until I opened it up and took out a handful of the weights. They seemed to symbolize all of the bullshit of the last several days. Not just the ridiculousness of being caught up in the middle of it, but the senselessness of the murder, the similarities of how we lived our lives, the fear of my own mortality, all of it. I came here because I wanted to slip away from everything, not only the life I had been living but also the memories of the life I'd given up before that. There was very little in the world that could offer me sanctuary. This had been one of those few places, short of finding a deserted island, building my own shelter and digging for water. Then I made the mistake of finding a dead body. Now I had this fifty pound bag of shit to remind me that what I wanted was never going to be possible.

The rest of the weights had slipped through my fingers, leaving behind a misshapen mass of lead that claimed to weigh four ounces. I knew it wouldn't change a thing, probably wouldn't even make me feel better, but I decided to take my frustrations out on it anyway. I threw it across the cabin and watched it slam into the wall before falling to the floor.

I was right. I felt no better and now probably had a small crack on my boat. But when I looked at where it had made contact, all I could see was a small smudge and a couple of flakes of silver paint.

I looked down at the sinker between my feet. It was definitely a little flatter on one side, and that side was no longer the color of lead.

It was the color of gold.

Chapter 46

Suddenly I felt very suspicious. I moved slowly, deliberately, as if any action too fast would get me shot. I leaned across the table and dragged the bag over towards me. I started shifting through the weights again, trying to separate them by size and weight. Most of them were small, fractions of an ounce, perfect for lake trout but worthless in the ocean. It shows you just how little I fish that I hadn't thought about the futility of such small weights out here before. A few were bigger, two ounces and up, but no matter which ones I picked up they were all flawless. There was no extra drop of paint, no fringe where it had dried improperly. Could I have picked the one fake weight in the bag? Hardly. My theory on coincidences has been very clearly spelled out

There was a small toolbox under one of the benches, and inside were a few leftover pieces of sandpaper from when I had refinished some of the woodwork. I picked one of the bigger weights and starts rubbing.

Yup. Thar's gold in this here bag.

Now it was all starting to make sense. Scooter, along with being an asshole, a rapist and a thief, was also a gold smuggler. He spent so much time on his boat away from people because he was perfecting his hobby. Maybe that was what he needed the money from Mike from, to stake a new claim, and maybe he was doing Mike a favor by driving him off from getting involved with these people. I don't know why it felt important to canonize the dead bastard, but suddenly I was trying to find the good in him, especially now that I imagined how his last days and weeks had gone down. If he had been the guy responsible for hiding the gold in plain sight by making it look like worthless fishing weights, he could have easily – albeit patiently – managed to skim a few grams here and there off of each shipment. It would have taken a long time to come up with fifty pounds, but it could be done.

Or maybe he wasn't patient. Maybe he was just a middleman, a weigh station between supplier and demander. Maybe he helped himself to a little to start, but when nobody caught him or said anything, he started to get bolder, more reckless, and helped himself to a big score. It's the plot of a thousand movies, all which have a bad ending. He tells his handlers he's been robbed, comes up with a story so crazy that he has to be believed, and creates the fake fishing weights to hide the gold and plan for his getaway. But the story starts to unravel, and before he can retire to his new life, the men he's double crossed come back to settle the score. And if he wasn't the only guy working for them, they'd definitely want his killing to set an example for anyone else in their enterprise that might be harboring such dreams.

I pictured him sitting there in his cabin, meticulously shaping the gold and painting each little piece, and I found myself laughing at the image of the people who had come looking for it using it as ballast for his corpse instead and never realizing it.

I also realized that corpse or not, at least the case was closed, and it was time for a vacation. I could explain it all to the Chief after I got back. I figured without a body, he couldn't be in too much of a hurry for answers anymore.

Chapter 47

Pop quiz; how many secret storage compartments do I have on my boat? Nice. You were paying attention. I kept each of the compartments separate, for just such an occasion as a Coast Guard boarding, but right now I wasn't looking for what had been on their mind, and I wasn't looking for a place to hide the bag. I simply tied it off and placed it under the table, the whole time multiplying twelve hundred dollars an ounce by fifty pounds.

My guess was that the mystery coroner was a nice guy as well as a trained killer and thought I would want a souvenir from my old friend. Somebody smarter than him, further up the food chain, might put two and two together however and if the boat had turned up empty for all the missing gold – which it obviously had – they would try to find where else it might have ended up. That would send them looking for me and my boat, and although it wasn't much to look at it, I'd rather it not suffer any more damage. Much like Scooter did, I simply left it hidden in plain sight.

Instead of hiding something there was something I was looking for. I stood in front of the stairs and ran my finger slowly across the top molding. The flaw that I was looking for was so perfect that it took me a few passes before I found it. I slipped my fingernail underneath it just so, moved it ever so slightly to the left, and voila!

Welcome to the first international bank of Richard Lockhart.

It had been international for many years, as I collected my pay in whatever was the local currency. Of course, as any first year econ major will tell you, many currencies have a tendency to not always be worth the same, especially when you're working with the unstable governments that had hired me in the first place. Back before I retired, it was convenient to have a little of everything, but as I knew my days were numbered I began converting it into the most stable paper I could. It doesn't matter what language you speak or what God you fight for, everyone likes pictures of Benjamin Franklin.

I know what you might be thinking too. I could use all this money, invest it in even the simplest account, and make that much more money. Possibly, but let me say there's a reason I have so many compartments. I could live to be a very old man and not come within a tenth of spending all that I already had. No need to make any more.

I grabbed a couple of stacks and threw them on the table where the gold had been sitting. Packing everything else I needed was easy, not only because life in the tropics means needing not much more than shorts, shirts and sandals, but also I was already packed. I simply unzipped my bag, hid the money deep in the middle of the clothes, and just like that I was ready to go.

Case closed, bags packed and a week or so in Bimini. I knew that I could stay out of sight enough that a threat wouldn't materialize. It was funny. Rachel's parents were afraid that everybody reminded them of somebody, and she couldn't figure out why I didn't do the same. It was easy enough to explain: I was the flip side of the coin. I remind somebody of everybody.

I'm the older brother of your first high school girlfriend. I'm the guy who gave the toast at a wedding you were a guest at. I'm the man that held the door for you, sat next to you at the football game, even had a beer or two with you at the bar. I enter your conscious and exit your memory before I ever register. I'm a phantom, and even if I came face to face with someone whose very life had depended on what I told him, and he wanted to return the favor by making me chum, he would most likely buy me a drink and never remember who I was.

For the first time since my nephew had woken me up five days ago, everything finally looked like it was going right for me. I grabbed the bag, wondered what her surprise was going to be for me, stepped up on the deck and felt my nuts grow cold.

The Chief had done exactly what I thought he could if he wanted to talk to me. He was standing there with two files in his hands.

Chapter 48

Maybe.

Maybe if I hadn't been involved in the fight at the bar last night.

Maybe if I wasn't excited about sailing away to Bimini, playing cabin boy and forgetting the last ninety-six hours.

Maybe if the Chief didn't have those two files in his hands and a worried look on his face.

Maybe if any one of these things hadn't been the reality as I stood on my deck that morning, I would have said "Great news, Chief. Turns out Scooter ran gold, got on the wrong side of some very bad people, and they were just settling the score. I don't have time to get into details now, but I promise I'll fill you in when I get back." Had I said that, things might have been different. But they weren't, because what I said was

"Chief?"

He eyed my bag. "Going somewhere?"

"Bimini for a week or so. Is that okay?"

He thought about it for a second. "Yeah, I guess so. I mean, as long as you think it is." He was obviously distracted by the paperwork in his hands and what it meant, so I hoped to clue him in and ensure my escape.

"I promise I'll be back in eight or nine days tops, so in case you need me to fill out paperwork or answer any questions about last night."

"Last night?"

Christ he was out of it. "The fight? Me and the south beach trio?"

His eyes flickered. "Oh, that, right. No, that's fine, that's...everything's settled from that. But yeah," he was getting lost again, "maybe you should get out of town for a few days."

Now he was making me nervous. "Am I in some sort of trouble that's not connected with all the trouble I've been in lately?"

"No, I don't...I don't think so. But best not to find out the hard way. A week should be good."

"Until whatever it is blows over?" But he spoke like he hadn't heard me.

"Are you taking your boat?"

"No, I'm sailing with Rachel. She's got work to do."

"Good, good. That way it'll look like you're still here." I gotta say, for bon voyage speeches, he was starting to make me feel like I'd booked passage on the Titanic and scheduled my rescue with the Lusitania. I was going to ask him what he meant by that and why he thought it would be important when he handed me the files he was carrying. "Read these while you're out on the open sea. It'll bring you up to speed on...um...Scooter."

That caught my ear. Not only had he somehow found out what Scooter's real name was, he had been focusing on it so much since I last talked to him that he had spaced on his nickname. "Hey, funny thing about Scooter. I should tell you what I discovered."

"Oh yeah? What's that?" He genuinely looked interested but also disgusted, as if he'd learned enough about Scooter to last him a while.

"Scooter got himself into league with some bad men, Chief, not the kind we should be handling on our own. Best I can tell is he's part of hundreds of pounds of gold going here and there. Definitely work for the FBI and other players outside your jurisdiction."

"If you think that's best." But he said it in a way that even he didn't believe.

"I thought you'd like that. Be able to wash your hands of it all."

"I suppose." He fingered the files so I would be sure to notice both of them. "But that won't get us any closer to solving either murder."

I laughed, hoping he wasn't really losing his mind. "Can't be two murders if there's only one body."

"You'd think that, wouldn't you? I mean, that's the logical sense to it all, isn't it?" Suddenly he became crystal clear. He wasn't distracted by thoughts and he wasn't going crazy. He was somewhere between terrified and pissed and trying to find a way to tell me why. "Of course, I don't know what to call it when the one body you find has the prints of one man and the ID of another."

"In the business we were in, I'd call it par for the course."

He looked up at me and his eyes held all those emotions. "It wasn't just a bonus, not with what came back with it on the search. If I had to bet who these guys actually thought they were killing, my money wouldn't be on the gold smuggler."

Out of the corner of my eye I could see Rachel waving me over. It was time for her to cast off, but he kept talking. "Let me ask you. You go out, you leave the boat, what kind of ID do you take with you?"

"My license, like normal people."

"Right. No need to worry about losing your passport."

"Is that the ID you found? It's as easy to fake one of those as a license. You know that." But he still wasn't listening.

"What if, though, when you were leaving, you weren't coming back. I mean the big 'never coming back.' What ID would you grab then?"

I knew what he meant so suddenly it took my breath away. If I knew I was cashing in, I would grab my passport, my original, and let me tell you friends and neighbors, it doesn't say Richard Lockhart. "This seems like even more of a reason to turn this over and get it out of your hair. I mean," and for no worthy reason, since we were the only two people in earshot, I dropped my voice down an octave, "do you really want to risk too much of who you are coming out during this investigation?"

"No. That's why I need it to be you to handle this."

"I wouldn't know where to begin."

"You will when you read the files." He began to pace, an outward sign of nervousness I'd never seen him manifest. "Look, you're right; I can't really make you do anything. I can't keep you from going to Bimini, I can't make you come back, and I can't make you follow through on this." He pressed the files against my chest so awkwardly I had to grab them. "We could hand it over, let the feds or the county take their best shot at it, and I can tell you right now the farthest they will get is creating a cold case file and forgetting about it. I'm not asking you to do this because you can do a better job, or because we need to get some measure of justice. I'm asking you to do it because you're the only person who can. And that includes me."

He made his speech and wasted no time getting on his dinghy. "Chief, believe me when I say nothing can change. Wherever Scooter is now, he's there alone, and the mystery coroner, the men in black and everyone else is out of our lives."

"No," he said, "I don't think so. But that's up to you to

decide for yourself."

I was feeling so good about the last thirty minutes and the next eight days I had forgotten that the Chief wasn't my friend, not by a long shot. "Is that because you know nothing will change? Just like you knew something would happen?"

He looked at me with the closest expression to fear I'd ever seen on his face. "Do you think I had something to do with all this?"

"The thought crossed my mind before, and right now it's back and bolder than ever."

"I'm not. Trust me when I say that right now that's about the only thing I am sure of." He pointed at the files. "You may have figured out some things that aren't in there, but believe me when I say there's more than you could imagine."

"I don't know, Chief. I can imagine a lot, and I've seen even more."

"Yeah, well, not like this." He pushed off and called over his shoulder. "You'll understand why I was damn lucky to have you end up with this after all." I could tell it wouldn't matter anything else I said, he was beyond listening. I could only watch him disappear before Rachel was back in my vision and now she was shrugging her shoulders and tapping her wrist.

Fuck him for building my curiosity. I almost thought to stop what I was doing and read them right then, but when I looked up she was unmooring her boat and getting ready to leave. Time's up, what's my final answer?

The distance between our boats was around fifty yards, and I was making probably about four knots. That gave me just under a half a minute to figure out what the hell was going on in my life. I hated working for him in the past and I had hated working for him this week, but those two hatreds combined wouldn't equal a tenth of the hate I would feel if I had to continue this relationship going forward. He knew that, he had to, and yet he still came out here to ask me to take the job. That alone should have told me my responsibilities were here on the island. If I needed a second opinion there was also the matter of these two files, at least one of which contained enough information to break an unbreakable man.

But at the same time it was all just another part of what I was trying to get away from. I had left his sight years before I retired for good, all that time slowly trying to find a way to purge the filth from my life and have a new way of living. There was no way anything this upsetting to him was going to not throw me right back into it. I could go back to my boat, clean out my bank, and Rachel and I would never have to be seen again. The only problem there was wondering if she could handle that kind of life, and if I could handle it with her.

I tied off on her stern and she leaned over the railing, fixing me with a smile so innocent and devilish I almost forgot I didn't know what I was doing. "I got nervous the Chief had reasons good enough to keep you here."

"He certainly made a very convincing argument."

"More convincing than this?" The balance of the smile shifted ever so slightly south and she stepped back just far enough so I knew to look at what she was wearing. It was another black outfit, this time a loose dress best suited for covering up while at the beach. When she knew she had my attention, she pulled it over her head.

The bathing suit she was barely wearing was the color of red every man dreams about. It doesn't matter how many different shades of various colors they make lipstick out of these days, there is nothing like that pure red that makes every man weak in the knees. I hadn't noticed that she had painted her lips and nails to match, and now that she was out of the dress I was too busy looking elsewhere to see them now either.

"Is this the surprise you were talking about?"

"Well, it was going to be." She made a show of reaching back for the dress. "But that's up to you, Tricky."

She leaned back over the railing, making sure what little fabric was in the top half of the suit strained against her flesh.

"Life's an adventure. You coming?"

THE END

Does he sail off with the beautiful woman or does he stay and solve the crime? Find out what happens next in

"Traitor Vic's Rum Punch."

Author's Notes & Acknowledgements

To repeat a joke I made earlier (and enjoy very much) I understand it takes a village to raise an idiot, and it was no different in this case. Several people have come forward to help me make this little novel of mine go from a note book – seriously, I started it as a side project just to give me some writing to do that didn't involve staring at the screen – to this pocket sized gem you are holding.

My good friend and partner in crime Chris Lang was generous in his time to not only read an earlier draft but also give me notes that helped tighten the action and refine the characters. The Surfpirate Bob Haslett is not only a talented graphic artist who brilliantly executed the ideas I had in my head to come up with a great cover design, he is also one hell of an MSWord tutor and helped me with the formatting of the text you just read. Kathleen Czerepak Ackerman is a friend I've known since childhood, and it is her four words that tell you what novel you are reading. And finally, as always, much thanks and love to Tamara Dower who keeps my website going.

Most novels have some sort of disclaimer that says "This is a work of fiction." I'm sure I should have included something like that, but one of the important characters is a talking manatee. Which means it should be pretty obvious that this is fiction. I bring this up for two reasons.

Terry

Reason number one is I don't know what the practices of the Coast Guard are when it comes to boarding a vessel looking for drugs, I'm not totally sure how peyote affects a person (nor if the described cure, including tequila, red wine, OJ, coffee, beer and an oyster would work) and I have no idea if shattering teeth sounds anything like breaking glass. I could have researched all of these things, but the fact is I make shit up. Besides if you know me, you know that one of my favorite sayings is "Never let the truth get in the way of a good story."

Reason number two is that while the work is fiction, some of the characters are not. I asked several of the local Key West musicians if I could use their names. The ones who said yes appear here in these pages, including one who asked I change one letter in his name. Next time you're in Key West, please check them out. They are an integral part of the fabric of the island. And if you've been there before, I'm sure you know where to find Barnacle Bob's and the Pelican Deck.

(Oh, and one other character. I had to ask him twice. Not because he said no the first time, but because I was having too much fun to remember the answer.)

Finally, if you've come this far, come a little farther. Check out my debut novel "Chasing Ghosts" available wherever unknown novels are found, including my aforementioned website: www.popcornjackterry.com

J-
New York
April 6th, 2016

stern and climbed up on deck, I could see the slight but important difference. To think of it in terms of paint, an albino's skin has a matte finish. This woman's skin, while certainly pale, had a semi-gloss like sheen to it, and it had nothing to do with sweat. Somehow she just seemed to glow.

She made no effort to introduce herself, so I made no hurry to push the point. I figured she was the stranger on a strange boat so the ball was in her court. I fixed myself a drink (which is a fancy way of saying I put some tequila and ice into a glass) and sat down opposite her.

After my shower (but unfortunately before I stuck my upper body in the ocean bobbing for corpses) I had dressed up reasonably nice by Key West standards. Compared to her, I was wearing a potato sack three sizes too large. Black isn't a color you see most people wear down here, but that was only part of what made her so distinctive. The way she wore the dress, the dress itself, made her seem extremely out of place, but she wore it with such confidence I noticed myself starting to feel unsettled. Maybe that was it. Maybe in New York she would be one of a million, but down here she was one in a million, and she knew it.

I wish I could say there was something vaguely familiar about her that helped me connect the dots and figure out why she was here, but instead it was good old deductive reasoning that gave me the answer. She wore a black dress, she had on black shoes, there was a black ribbon holding back her hair, and even her glasses had black frames. She probably felt like she didn't have to introduce herself since we had already met a couple of nights ago.

And she had left her black panties behind.

Her legs were crossed and her dress stopped just north of her knees. I don't know what made me think they were her